MW01614848

DIRTY LIKE US

JAINE DIAMOND

Dirty Like Us
Jaine Diamond

Copyright © 2016 Jaine Diamond

All rights reserved.

No part of this book may be reproduced, scanned, uploaded or distributed in any manner whatsoever without written permission from the publisher, except in the case of brief quotation embodied in book reviews.

This book is a work of fiction. Names, characters, places and incidents are the product of the author's imagination or are used fictitiously. Any resemblance to actual events, locales, organizations or persons is coincidental.

Published by DreamWarp Publishing Ltd.
www.jainediamond.com

Cover Design: DreamWarp Publishing Ltd.

Dirty Like Us

For my man;
you're more of a romantic than you think.

Author's Note

This book, *Dirty Like Us*, is a prequel novella for the Dirty series. As a prequel, this is a cliffhanger book—*Dirty Like Us* is Zane and Maggie's story, but it's only a slice of their story. These two have a complicated relationship, and there is so much more to their story than could possibly fit into a novella. This is not an easy love, and it's bound to go so very wrong before it goes right... All of which means that Zane and Maggie's story won't be continued and resolved until later in the series, when they get their own full-length novel (*Dirty Like Zane*).

In the meantime, *Dirty Like Us* gives us a delicious taste of what's going on between these two!

With love from the beautiful west coast of Canada (the home of Dirty!),

Jaine

Prologue

Maggie

The red carpet was worn beneath our feet. The altar was a single step, also carpeted in red, on which we stood, along with the officiant.

The officiant wore a black leather motorcycle jacket, a faded Steppenwolf T-shirt, ratty jeans and biker boots. A black leather bible decorated with silver studs lay open on his hands.

I wore a pink dress.

The room was small, and there were no windows. The ceiling was arched and the walls were black, strewn with neon beer signs and replica platinum albums.

There was a row of eight gunmetal chairs, four to the right of the aisle and four to the left, two of which were occupied. A woman I didn't know stood at the back of the room with a polite smile on her face. A man with a gun stood guard at the door.

Outside, traffic rumbled by, occasionally vibrating the kitschy junk on the walls.

In the next room, an awful song played faintly on repeat. A cheesy, sleazy rock song about a schoolgirl.

Near me, someone was talking.

But all I could hear was that old Steppenwolf song, "Magic Carpet Ride," playing in my head. I heard it the way Zane once sang it, as we sat around a campfire drinking Jäger from a bottle someone passed around, his voice so raw and smoky and beautiful it gave me goosebumps. I heard it the way my mom used to play it, loud, on her wonky old turntable, as she danced in the kitchen in one of her flowy blouses and a pair of cut-offs.

I could see her now, dancing in her bare feet, and looking so, so young.

And I wished she was here.

I was holding hands with him, and my knees were quivering. I could feel his heartbeat in his fingers wrapped tight around mine. His thumb smoothed back and forth across my knuckles, over the new ring on my finger, as I breathed, shallow and slow.

He was looking at me. I knew he was. I could feel the heat of his gaze moving over my face.

"Maggie."

I took a breath and felt his heartbeat, once… twice… Then I looked up into that gorgeous face. His arctic blue eyes held mine. He squeezed my hands slightly.

Zane.

Me.

Holding hands at the altar.

Holy shit.

"That's your cue, babe," Zane said, and I realized the man in the leather jacket had been the one speaking. To me. Everyone was looking at me and waiting.

And I just stared at Zane.

The corners of his eyes twitched. He smiled slightly and I couldn't stop myself. I never could, when it came to him.

I smiled back.

"Yeah," I said, in response to the man's question, but the word cracked and came out a whisper. I cleared my throat and found my voice. "I do."

Chapter One

Maggie

Two hours earlier…

I stood in the middle of the massive, glittering bathroom, trying not to imagine how much this hotel suite would've cost if we had to pay for it. And trying not to think about why we didn't.

I'd told Coop to go ahead and help himself to the complimentary champagne, because no way I was drinking it. Instead I grabbed one of the little glasses by the sink and fixed myself a vodka cran, pouring from the bottle of Stoli I'd paid for myself. Then I lay my travel case open on the floor and took a breath.

The last hour of my life had been a total gong show, the conversation with my father pretty much the furthest thing from an aphrodisiac. I just needed a few minutes to get my head together and switch gears.

I took a swig of my drink and assessed myself in the mirrored wall. I was still wearing the jeans and midriff-baring jacket I'd worn to dinner with the crew, but I'd already decided the occasion called for something a *lot* sexier.

I dug through my stuff, unearthing the new lingerie and snapping off the tags. Then I went over my mental checklist as I got undressed.

The band was all settled into the hotel, finished with the promotional interviews I'd set up for them earlier in the day, and they were officially set loose for the night. In Las Vegas. The last I'd seen of each of them, they were off in various directions in search of sex (Zane), booze (Dylan), and/or solitude (Jesse and Elle). Tomorrow night was the final show of the tour and everyone was jacked up on a hazardous cocktail of anticipation, adrenaline and hormones. Not the kind of hazard I could do much about, other than stay out of the way and be on hand for cleanup later. My boss, Brody, and I were band management, which meant we booked gigs, made sure everyone got paid, and generally kept the money flowing in. But it also meant we took it upon ourselves to make sure everyone stayed relatively sane, so the reality was, if anything fell apart between now and tomorrow's show, my phone was gonna blow up like the Freemont Street light show, and not like I could ignore it.

Story of my life, but at least everything was as it should be on that front.

Security, crew, and gear were all accounted for and everything was set for Dirty, hottest rock band on the planet and my kickass employers—fuck, yeah—to rock the hell out of the new arena on the Vegas Strip. And while I was excited about tomorrow's show in that bittersweet way that marked the end of each tour, I was really looking forward to a momentary diversion from the madness.

A diversion of the sexual variety. Because the Penny Pushers were also in town for the show, and that meant I was hooking up.

I slipped into the skimpy lace babydoll and matching thong, both a vibrant lime-green that looked amazing against my complexion. Thanks to my mom, I had flawless light-brown skin, which I'd always considered my best feature. Admittedly, because it made me look less like my dad. Usually when people found out who he was, they assumed I'd *want* to be associated with him. He was rich and famous, after all. But those were the people who'd never met him.

I took a couple more swigs of my drink, hiked up my cleavage with the stiff demi cups of the babydoll, and touched up my makeup, letting the liquor and the bizarre, hyper-reality of this moment soak in.

I, Maggie Omura, was about to fuck a rock star.

What would you think of that one, Mom?

She'd laugh, I figured. Hard. Since this went completely against The Rule.

I'd made up The Rule myself when I first came to work for Dirty six years ago. Actually, I'd made up many rules. What the hell did I know? I was a nerdy, idealistic nineteen-year-old with stars in my eyes. But as I'd discovered, in the total shit storm of rock 'n' roll chaos that soon became my life, there was only one rule that warranted keeping.

No Screwing The Talent.

When I first met Dirty, their debut album had just incinerated the charts and they were coming off their first world tour. I was naive and inexperienced, but I had a head for business and all I'd ever wanted to do was work in the music industry. I managed to get an incredibly tenuous foot in the door merely because of a lucky-horseshoe-up-the-ass situation—I happened to have a class with Dirty guitarist Jesse Mayes's sister in college, and she and I had become friends. I also had the hugest, stupidest puppy-love crush on Zane Traynor, blond bad boy and lunatic lead singer... and when he set his ice-blue eyes on me, I knew the only way I wouldn't fuck everything up was by eating, sleeping and breathing The Rule.

Over the years, The Rule had kept me out of trouble. A *lot* of trouble. However. Sometimes rules became outdated. Needed a little revising. Or strategic bending.

And since I wasn't about to screw a member of the band I worked for, it didn't totally count, right?

"Maggie?" Coop tapped on the frosted-glass bathroom door, amusement and a touch of concern in his voice. "You ever coming out?" He also sounded horny, his voice low and a little huskier than usual.

Perfect.

I stood back to check my work and felt ridiculously sexy for about five seconds, knowing he was gonna love it... until it really dawned on me that I'd bought the lingerie for that reason. Because Andy Cooper had mentioned, months ago, that I looked hot in this color. Which meant... yeah. I was putting way too much effort into this.

Kinda like I did with every-fucking-thing.

But this was weird, right? Crossing a line?

Coop was just a hookup, and no sane woman bought hot, expensive lingerie just for some guy she was hooking up with unless she was looking to turn that hookup sex into hang-out-afterward-and-do-it-again sex, followed by wake-up-together-the-next-morning-and-do-it-yet-again sex.

And I definitely wasn't looking for that.

Was I?

I smoothed my long, dark hair and chewed my lip at my reflection. Hot. But yeah, weird.

"Maggie?" Coop knocked again.

I pounded back the rest of my drink. "Coming."

Lingerie or no? I could take it off, walk out there naked.

Veto.

Put the jeans back on?

I made an executive decision to go with the lingerie, took a deep breath, and opened the door. Despite the fact that I didn't feel quite as special about Coop as the lingerie implied, my night had just gone to hell and I *really* needed this distraction.

I just hoped he had time to help me blow off all this steam; it could take a while.

Coop stood back, his eyebrows raising as he drank me in. He wore a vintage Sex Pistols T-shirt with the sleeves cut off, showing off his incredibly decent arms, with gray jeans and a studded belt. His blond hair was tousled to shit, like it always was, and an impish smile broke out on his face. "Whoa. Maggie... shit." He scrubbed his hand through his hair. "I feel kinda underdressed."

"Then let's get you undressed," I said, letting my inner slut take over as I grabbed him by his shirt and pulled him over to the giant bed. I'd claimed the smaller of the two bedrooms in the penthouse suite, yet the bed was king size, which made me wonder what was in the master bedroom. Harem size?

Fitting, given who'd be sleeping in it.

Don't even go there.

I yanked Coop against me and we came together in a hungry, slightly awkward kiss. He pushed me back onto the bed, his warm weight settling over me. Despite the offer of free champagne, he tasted vaguely like beer, which reminded me of finding him in the hotel bar half an hour ago... which reminded me of running into Zane about half an hour before that—

Do. NOT. Go. There.

Coop's body was lean and hard as he ground himself against me, his hips dragging over mine, the hard ridge of the unmistakable erection in his jeans setting off sparks of pleasure between my legs, and I gasped.

Oh, *hell* yes... this was exactly what I needed.

He kissed his way down my neck and I groaned, arching my back, getting into it as he sucked on my throat—

Holy. Shit. I stiffened as joyful screaming and laughter erupted in the room next door—the main room of the penthouse suite.

The voices of multiple women.

Coop didn't seem to notice. Or care. He just ground his hard dick against me and kissed me again. I shut my eyes as his weight pressed me down, his hips moving faster against me, his body heating up. He grabbed my breast, squeezing hard, and sank his tongue deep in my mouth.

Then I heard it. I heard *him*. My "roommate" for the night. His smoky voice so close outside the bedroom door I cringed.

My eyes flew open. I ripped away, stopping Coop with a hand on his chest, so suddenly I startled us both.

He looked down at my hand as I panted beneath him. "You okay?" he asked, disoriented. "Did I hurt you?"

"No," I managed to choke out, clearing my throat.

Fuck. Me.

My head was spinning, and I could still hear his voice in the other room. I couldn't tell what he was saying, but I knew that cocky timber. I knew the sound of Zane Traynor working his magic on a bunch of women.

"Just… don't…" I gasped out, shaking my head, "… don't stop." Then I grabbed Coop by his neck and smashed my mouth to his as a ridiculous wave of guilt crashed through me.

I didn't feel guilty about breaking The Rule. I'd been breaking it with Coop on a casual but semi-regular basis for a while now.

I felt guilty I wasn't breaking it with *him*.

Yeah. That was the messed-up truth of it. Because I'd always secretly fantasized that if I was ever going to break The Rule I'd do it balls to the wall, in a total blaze of glory, me and the ice-blue-eyed reigning god of rock—and cock—swinging from chandeliers and breaking furniture.

But thank God my mother didn't raise that kind of fool.

I, Maggie Omura, was never going to let my incredibly

misguided lady parts lead me to Zane Traynor's bed. No matter how much they might want me to.

That way lies madness.

On the other hand, Andy Cooper, wickedly talented bass player for the Penny Pushers and genuinely nice guy, was worth breaking a rule for, right? Besides that, Coop was exactly my type. Which was tall, blond, and rock 'n' roll.

Also, he'd just torn off his shirt and tossed it on the floor, and the sight of his bare chest helped me to focus.

He yanked the babydoll over my head and tossed it somewhere across the room as I tried really, really hard to block out the sounds of screeches and giggles from next door. I was pretty sure Coop said a bunch of nice things about how sexy I was as he kissed his way down my body, but I didn't really hear it.

Instead, I heard Zane's laugh. That potent, sexy-ass, full-on Viking laugh I would know anywhere, had creamed my panties to enough times that I'd never be able to hear it and not get wet. It was like a goddamn Pavlovian response.

I wriggled uncomfortably as Coop ran his fingers down between my legs, skimming the lace of my thong, hyper-aware of the fact that I was more turned on by that laugh than the feel of Coop's touch on my body. He rubbed me up and down, his hand moving in small, eager circles as he kissed his way down my stomach… and I tried to enjoy it, I really did.

But then the music kicked in.

Loud.

It was Guns N' Roses, "You're Crazy," at top fucking volume. Not the acoustic version. The heavy version, hard and fast, thumping through the wall.

Coop looked up in a lust daze, the corner of his mouth hooking in a slight smile. "Who's out there?"

"Just… ah… one of the guys…" I said, my brain split between the pleasure of what he was doing to me and the party going on next door. "And... about... half a chorus line... from the sound of it..."

Coop laughed. "Should I go tell them to turn it down?"

Sweet. But no way I would do that to Coop.

"No," I said, "just keep..." and then my head dropped back on the bed as he increased the urgency of his touch. He swirled his tongue around my navel, letting out a low groan, then kissed his way down. I took a breath and struggled to focus on the sensations of his tongue licking its way along the lacy edge of my thong, his fingers slipping inside to peel back the fabric. Then I felt the caress of his hot breath, just as laughter exploded on the other side of the wall.

His laughter, loud and cocksure.

A chorus of female giggles followed, and a surge of raw jealousy scorched through me.

Worst. Roommate. *Ever.*

Would it totally kill the mood if I put in earplugs before Coop fucked me?

Yes. Yes, it would.

Maybe we could put on some music of our own? I had a laptop here somewhere... but no way my laptop speakers could compete with the sound system from hell next door.

Zane laughed again, and my nipples pricked.

I clenched my teeth and squirmed in frustration.

Maybe my father was right.

Maybe I was just some glorified groupie.

God knew I'd had it bad for Zane since long before I'd met him in the flesh. And ever since... yeah, I still lusted after him— in secret. Physically speaking, Zane Traynor was a god among men, and I was only human.

But that didn't mean I'd ever, ever act on it.

Screw him, said the voice of reason in my head, the one that

12

sounded suspiciously like my mom's. Because what the hell did my dad know about it anyway?

No mere groupie would've worked as hard as I had, for as long as I had, and put up with the shit that I had—much less stuck to The Rule for as many years as I did.

And now that I'd chosen to break The Rule? So what? I was a single woman. It was my prerogative if I wanted to screw every rock star I'd ever met. Besides, I was having a great time with Coop, I was ignoring Zane's inconvenient presence, and I wasn't at all imagining that it was his face between my legs right now.

Yeah.

I totally was.

Good news, though: I'd completely tensed up and my hand was on Coop's forehead. I was tongue-blocking him.

Sexy.

He stopped, obviously, and looked up at me. "Uh... are you sure—?"

"Hang on a sec, while I commit a super quick murder."

He backed off, letting me up.

"You sure you don't want me to—?"

"Nope." I rolled over and off the bed in one angry lunge, righting my lime-green thong. "I've got this." I scooped up the first thing I saw—his giant T-shirt—and thrust my almost-naked self into it as I stalked over to the bedroom door.

When I threw it open, the scene that greeted me was pretty much what it sounded like.

The main room of the penthouse suite had been overrun with groupies, bits of their skimpy clothing flung across the gaudy, oversized furniture. There were five of them, and while I doubted they were actual strippers—Zane didn't tend to hang with women who expected to get more attention than they gave, since he preferred to be the center of attention in any given room—I'd definitely walked in on some kind of amateur revue for their one-man audience.

Two blonds were dancing together on the coffee table, the one with the big fake breasts, already topless, undressing the other.

A chick with jet-black hair, in a metallic shrink-wrap dress, was bent over in the kitchen snorting what I could only assume was cocaine off the glossy countertop, showing off her matching metallic thong while she did it.

The other two were pawing each other on one of the big, plush couches. And there was Zane, front row center. Sprawled back on that same couch, legs spread wide. The girls were kneeling over him, and I really could've sworn he looked kinda bored as he watched them make out.

I was already bored, but then again, I didn't have a penis.

One of the girls in his lap was a redhead. The other looked suspiciously Filipina, and even though she didn't look much like *me*, it really fucking irritated me. The man had a serious talent for irritating me—and for sniffing out exactly when he was doing it, like some sadistic bloodhound. I was pretty sure he got off on it. It didn't surprise me at all when his ice-blue eyes met mine, though none of the girls even noticed I was there.

He stared at me, his eyes flaring. He looked pretty blown away to see me, actually. Well, no shit.

Not like I *wanted* to be stuck in the room adjoining his latest orgy.

I pointed one finger at him and rolled it back, in the universal gesture for *Get your ass over here*. Which he could've ignored. He could've told me where to go with a finger gesture of his own.

Technically, the man was my employer.

Instead he dumped the girls off his lap, eyes still locked on mine, and adjusted himself in his low-slung jeans. That's when I made the mistake of glancing down.

The top button of his jeans was undone, showing a triangle of sun-kissed skin and a hint of his golden treasure trail, not to mention the perfect, tight abs that disappeared under his shirt.

The girls kept going at it, oblivious to his departure, as he rose and stalked toward me.

Tall. Blond. And *very* rock 'n' roll.

I just watched him, my features carefully arranged in a look of cool, unruffled displeasure as I forced myself to keep breathing so my heart wouldn't explode in an epic cataclysm of rage and repressed lust. Luckily, I had a *lot* of practice with this. Still, my traitorous gaze wandered down the thin black T-shirt stretched over his broad, hard chest and the badass black leather vest, the muscles bunching in his sleek, California-tanned arms... the unbuttoned jeans just barely clinging to his hips... and *fuck*... did it make me a total weirdo that I had a crazy weakness for the man's bare feet?

It didn't exactly escape my notice that his dick looked pretty hard, either. Kinda like it was about to punch through his jeans, but Zane's package pretty much always looked that way.

It wasn't exactly an industry secret that Zane Traynor was well-hung.

In fact, I'd seen his naked cock with my own eyes, multiple times. Not that that meant anything. Pretty sure everyone and their dog had seen it. Since the man was Adonis incarnate, you couldn't even blame him for showing it off, though his habit of walking around naked in mixed company—irritating for a multitude of reasons—was the main reason everyone in the band refused to share a suite with him.

Well that, and all the groupies.

Really, you'd think a decade would be plenty of time for your average man to tire, or bore, of the groupie thing and move on. Zane, though?

Nothing was average about Zane.

He stopped a few inches from me, all up in my space, but I

stood my ground. I looked straight up into his beautiful face and met his unholy blue eyes.

His blond hair, shaved short on the sides but long on top, slid over his eye as he looked down at me. He raked it slowly back with one ring-laden hand and I caught a breath of him... that crazy-delicious man scent of his that always made my ovaries skip a beat.

"Maggie May," he said, and the devil was in his slow, easy smile. Yeah. The son of a bitch smiled, like he was happy to see me. "Just thinking about you."

Fuck me. He totally said that.

He eyed the oversized T-shirt I was wearing, the diabolical gears turning in his head. "The hell are you doing here?"

I wasn't gonna touch that. Not the point. Though I *was* glad to hear that he didn't know I was in the next room when he decided to throw this little party.

Then the song changed, and Marvin Gaye's "Let's Get It On" started playing... and the bottom completely fell out of my anger. Because seriously.

"Classy, Zane."

"I'm all class, sweetheart," he said, and the smile lit up his gorgeous face.

I couldn't even help smiling back as I rolled my eyes. *Shit*, though. I was supposed to be mad.

How the hell did he always do this to me?

Oh, right. Because the man was evil.

He was also charming as hell, and while I wanted to hate him, a lot, sometimes I failed at that. Big time.

Sometimes—well, most of the time—I liked Zane Traynor far too much for my own good.

Chapter Two

Zane

Maggie crossed her arms and glared up at me, like she was trying really hard to stay pissed. Which was cool with me. When Maggie got pissed, I got hard. Which meant I was already a helluva lot harder than I was a minute ago watching a couple of random chicks suck face. Especially when her nipples popped out against her shirt.

I did kinda feel like a jackass though. Had no clue she was in there.

My gaze skimmed down the oversized Sex Pistols shirt she was wearing, obviously a dude's. Not Maggie's usual look. Her lips were swollen and her compulsively-smooth hair was mussed up like she'd just gotten something on her back besides sleep.

What the hell did I interrupt in there?

I glanced over her shoulder but I couldn't see shit, just the door to a bathroom. I shifted closer until we almost touched, leaning a shoulder on the door frame.

"Who the fuck's been sucking on your neck?" My gaze had snagged on the mark I was pretty sure was a hickey.

She made an exasperated, frustrated noise in her throat that made my balls pull up tight.

It was no secret, at least to my dick, that I wanted this woman. Unfortunately for me and my dick, I'd never gotten my hands on her for more than a hug.

Maggie and I were "coworkers" and "friends" and not supposed to "go there."

According to her.

"Zane," she said extra-politely, "please take this in the nicest way possible, but you need to fuck off right now."

I ignored that. Maggie told me to fuck off at least once a day. Justifiably.

We had that kind of relationship. I was comfortable enough to piss her off, she was comfortable enough to tell me to fuck off, and at the end of the day none of it mattered. Maggie and I *were* friends. The kind that occasionally wanted to kill each other, but still.

What kind of friend would I be if I didn't at least make sure she wasn't in there with some loser?

I tried to get a look behind her again but she closed the door as far as she could, wedging herself in the narrow opening. I wedged myself right in with her, shouldering the door a little farther open. I drew the line at forcing my way past her, but fuck yeah. I was gonna check up on this asshole whether she liked it or not.

"Come on, Maggs. I wanna meet him." I gave her my wickedest smile, the one that made most girls soak their panties.

Maggie? Maggie wasn't most girls.

"Don't be an asshole, Zane. And would you please mind banging your new lady friends in your own room? You've got the master bedroom. See, over there. Behind those nice big solid doors."

"Oh, they're not for me."

She rolled her eyes. "Right."

"I brought them for Jesse," I said, which was true, even if she didn't believe it. "Hear he and Elle are fighting."

Yeah, so I was a shit disturber. But when weren't those two fighting?

Fuck if getting together wasn't the worst mistake my two dumbass bandmates ever made. I'd put money on a breakup at the end of this tour. Better for the band. Better for everyone.

Loved Elle, she was a great girl, but my band brother needed an epic cocksuck, badly, to remind him life was too short for one pussy. Especially one that drove him up the fucking wall.

"Well," Maggie said, "I'm sure Jesse *and Elle* would appreciate the gesture, but Jesse isn't here. I am."

"Cool. And why is that?"

She sighed. "Let's just say... things got screwed up with the rooms, okay?" Then she started chewing on her lip.

"Uh-huh," I said, distracted at the sight of her teeth gnawing on that full bottom lip. Fuck, but Maggie had a hot mouth. "Screwed up how?"

What the fuck happened to this girl's mood since I saw her in the lobby an hour ago, looking all flushed and fucking cheerful? It was a great look on her, and I wanted some of it. I'd gotten a little carried away, putting her up against the wall, and for a nanosecond as those gorgeous gray eyes blinked up at me I thought she might actually accept my invitation to come party, which she never did. I always asked. She always said no.

It was kind of a ritual.

Maybe for once I shouldn't have taken it like a gentleman.

"Look, it sucks we have to share a suite," she said, ignoring my question. "But we're both gonna do what we're gonna do." She cocked her head a little, glancing past me. "Seriously though, can we draw the line at the coke?"

I waited until her gray eyes lifted to mine again. I didn't love seeing the worry in them… but Maggie *always* worried about me falling off the wagon into a vat of whiskey. I got that. Cocaine was never my thing, but Jack Daniels wasn't exactly a hard man to find in a Vegas hotel.

Then I gave her what she wanted, because yeah. It was Maggie. And I was pussy-whipped like that.

"Yo, Snow White," I called over to the black-haired chick in the kitchen. "Time to go, sweetheart."

She was dancing by herself to Marvin Gaye, but Natalie jumped down off the coffee table, dragging the other blond with her to form a protective wall of bitch. "What!" Nat squawked, then threw me a theatrical pout. "If she goes then so do we."

"Then go," I said.

"Zane! What the fuck! Who the fuck is *she?*" Nat stood there in her panties, totally fucking indignant, looking at Maggie like she'd just stepped in shit.

Which really cranked up my stone cold.

"Get your skank ass outta here, Nat."

Natalie's mouth fell open. It was a good mouth to have around if you wanted your cock sucked, but other than that, she could keep it shut as far as I was concerned. She was the only one of them I'd met before half an hour ago, and that wasn't exactly a ringing endorsement for the rest.

"You're a real asshole," she snapped, yanking on her skirt.

"So they keep telling me."

Nat huffed, grabbed the rest of her clothes and stalked out with her coked-up friend. The other blond yanked a top over her fake tits, kissed me on the cheek, gave Maggie a catty once-over and left.

"Don't let the door smack your ass on the way out!" Maggie called after her, then grumbled, "Wouldn't wanna give it chlamydia."

I stared at Maggie and she gave me a fake-ass smile right back.

So fucking interesting.

Six years I'd known her, and I'd never seen her in this particular mood. Normally she kept her shit under wraps. Cool, controlled Maggie; it wasn't easy, even for me, to faze the woman. But right now, she was definitely pissed the fuck off, and frustrated.

Sexually frustrated?

If I didn't know better, I might've even said she was jealous.

Whatever it was, it was giving me a raging hard-on.

She made an irritated noise in her throat and I followed her gaze; the other two chicks were still at it on the couch, but now they were horizontal and kinda scissoring.

"Good night, Zane."

Maggie tried to shut the door, but I stopped it with my foot.

"Aren't we in a mood."

"Hey." Some shirtless dickwit appeared behind Maggie, running a hand through his scraggly hair, and a flash of kill-crazy jealousy went off like a firecracker in my gut. "Everything okay?" He met my eyes and flicked his chin at me in greeting.

Fucking *Coop*.

I blinked, 'cause I couldn't quite believe it.

Maggie was fucking *Coop*?

Shit, no.

I was all for fucking, in general. Was even pretty sure on a rare occasion or two some fuckwad had probably slipped under my nose and snaked his way up Maggie's skirt. I was no idiot. Chick as hot as Maggie had gotten cock somewhere, at some point in history, even if she was too fucking discreet, not to mention uptight, to ever let on about it.

But this? Not happening.

So fucking not happening.

"Give us a minute," she said to him sweetly, like really fucking sweetly, in a tone I'd sure as fuck never heard her use on me. "You know, band business."

"Oh. Sure." Coop disappeared, reluctantly. No shit. I'd get impatient too if Maggie was talking to some asshole at the door instead of riding my dick.

"You're not fucking Coop," I said, low enough he wouldn't hear it, leaning in to make sure she did, my face tipped down to hers.

She didn't back down. She just glowered at me, her eyes narrowing and her sweet mouth puckering, all pissed off and petite.

Which was why I loved fighting with Maggie. She was so fucking hot when she was mad. Hot, and cute as all fuck. Adorable. Like a feral kitten.

Also, if I really hit the sweet spot and she lost her temper, made it a lot harder for her to ignore me like she usually tried to do when I jabbed her buttons.

"Are you fucking Coop?" I pressed.

"News flash, Zane," she bit out. "You're not the only one who might want to do it in this stupid-fancy hotel suite, okay?"

"Jesus, though. *Coop*?"

She glared up at me, a storm brewing in her gray eyes. Then she growled. She actually *growled*, low in her throat, and I swear to Christ I almost came in my pants. "What the hell is wrong with Coop?"

"Where do you want me to start? For one, he's not me."

"Nuh-uh," she said, pinching the bridge of her nose. "Not doing this. Not getting into this with you."

"Let's get into it," I said, pushing another inch into the room, my pulse beating in my dick, spurring me on.

"Nope." She put her hand in the middle of my chest, holding

me off. "It's been a really bad night, I have not been laid since Christmas, and you are *not* going to ruin this for me."

Then she shut the door in my face.

———

Christmas?

Christmas was four months ago.

As I stood there, my back to the bedroom door, I racked my fucking brain to figure out who the hell Maggie'd fucked at Christmas.

Coop?

Some other fuckwit?

As far as I knew she wasn't seeing anyone regular. Maggie'd never had a boyfriend in the years I'd known her. I'd seen Coop checking her out. I'd seen him flirt with her, but big fucking deal. Who didn't flirt with Maggie? Half the crew was hard up for her, but the girl was so fucking proper and all-business she hardly seemed to notice. She so rarely partied with anyone, I'd gotten pretty comfortable telling myself if she wasn't sucking my cock, at least she wasn't sucking anyone else's.

Now I had a visual. Sweet Maggie, down on her knees sucking off Andy Cooper—*fuuuck*. The murderous surge of testosterone and adrenalin made my dick so hard it felt like it might split in half.

Shit.

Maybe I *was* a fucking idiot.

Two hot chicks, horny and willing, were going at it right in front of me, and my head was in the next room.

But no fucking wonder. I'd been hot for Maggie, one of a very few woman I'd ever spent more than an hour with who wouldn't spread her legs for me, for years. *Years.* And now she was giving it up to Coop?

23

Fuck. That.

Who the hell did he think he was?

Asshole had pretty much fucked his band's sweet ride on Dirty's coattails the second he breathed on Maggie. I said the word, the Pushers were off the next tour, and that gave me a grim fucking sense of satisfaction.

Would I actually do it? Maybe.

Depending how things went down tonight.

I grabbed the remote to lower the volume on the music. Too bad. It was Wolfmother's "Woman," a decent song to fuck to.

I liked sex the way I liked my music: loud and hard.

No idea how Marvin Gaye got in the mix. Probably my wise-ass drummer, fucking with me.

I listened, but I couldn't hear shit from next door. What kind of awkwardly quiet, polite sex were those two planning on having? What were they doing in there, right now?

And how long was I gonna let this slide?

According to my phone, three fucking minutes had passed since Maggie shut the door. Felt like a goddamn hour.

But the longer I let this go, the worse it would be for Coop when I kicked his ass out. Yeah, so I was a sadistic prick. Didn't bother me in the slightest that I was about to cockblock a brother.

Not when he was in there right now with Maggie, getting ready to stick his dick in her.

Right. That was about far enough.

I hammered my fist on the bedroom door. Hard.

Half a minute later, Coop opened it.

"Maggie!" I thundered over him. "Get your ass out here."

"Don't let him in!" Maggie called from inside. "He's like a goddamn vampire. You invite him in, you give him power."

Coop's eyes narrowed a little as he looked me over and every muscle in my body coiled tight. Pretty sure he could smell the lust and aggravation rolling off me, but he just shrugged. "Sorry, man."

He started to close the door but I stopped it with my hand.

"Coming in to talk to Maggie," I said evenly. "You can step aside or I can take this shit right through you."

He sized me up again and I flexed my other hand at my side, a couple of knuckles cracking as I made a fist. Adrenalin surged through me. Never woulda thought Coop had it in him, but shit. Was he actually considering fighting me for Maggie?

I'd spent years as a kid getting the shit kicked outta me by dudes way tougher and way meaner than Coop, and you got a clue, you lose enough fights, eventually you learn how to win. Which meant Coop took me on, he was so gonna lose this fight.

He knew it, too.

"Whatever," he muttered and opened the door.

"For fuck's sake, Zane!" Maggie scrambled off the bed, yanking her shirt down to cover herself. She was still wearing Coop's T-shirt. "What do you want?"

"Want?" I met her in the middle of the room and once I was in her face, I leveled her with a hard, simmering eye-fuck, seeing as that was the only way I ever got to fuck her. "You really want an answer to that, babe?"

"You two got some shit to sort out?" Coop asked, standing off to the side, scrubbing a hand through his hair.

"Yup," I said, in the exact same breath that she said, "No."

We stood there a foot apart, me eye-fucking her and vibrating with adrenalin, my dick standing at attention, her glaring up at me with her chest heaving and not blinking.

"Yeah, I'm just gonna go."

"Cool," I said, as Coop headed for the door. "Coupla girls in the other room. They're yours if you want. Just take 'em with you when you go."

"Alright, brother."

Maggie's jaw dropped.

"Andy." She looked from me to him as he paused in the doorway. Then she walked over to him. "I have your *shirt*," she said, clearly unable to process what the fuck was going on.

"Keep it," he said. Then he gave her a chaste little kiss on the forehead and left, shutting the door behind himself.

Maggie drew a deep, ragged breath, then let it out between her clenched teeth. Her shoulders dropped as she turned to me.

"Are you kidding me?"

I shrugged. "He scares easy, Maggs. And he was pretty quick to replace you. Better you find that out now."

She stood there raging, kinda like a baby bull about to charge. Then she took a few slow, measured breaths. She walked over and stood in front of me. Her gray eyes met mine, so fucking stunning against her honey-toned skin.

"I hope that amused you. Because it really fucking sucked for me."

"Maggie—"

"Don't. Coop's a nice guy, and you just treated him like—"

"Coop's a fucking pussy," I ground out. "He just *walked out on you*. While you're wearing his shirt. And why don't you take that shit off? Take a shower while you're at it, 'cause you stink like smarmy bass player."

Yup.

Shit disturber.

But some things just needed to be said.

Maggie stared at me and an ugly, loaded, fucking terrible silence landed in the wake of my words. Her lips parted... then she shut her mouth. Her jaw spasmed, her eyelashes trembled, and for a horrible minute I thought she might cry.

Then she scowled instead and something raw flashed in her eyes, between hurt and rage.

"Yeah?" She whipped the shirt off over her head and flung it across the room. "Well, the shirt's not the only thing he touched." She stood there in her tiny, neon-green panties and nothing else, and my jaw went slack.

I had no words.

No. Fucking. Words.

I'd never seen so much of Maggie before. Couldn't believe how much better the flesh was than my imagination, and I'd spent a helluva lot of time imagining her.

I drank in her petite curves, the soft swell of her breasts, her hard nipples a dark, dusky pink as her chest rose and fell with the force of her uneven breaths.

Then I swallowed, hard, and ground my teeth. I shoved my hands in the pockets of my jeans.

Had to, or I was gonna grab her, slam her down on the bed and devour every inch of that gorgeous smooth skin.

"Guess I should take this off too." She plucked at the see-through lace of her panties and my dick achieved a new level of hard, kinda like reinforced steel. Then her finger touched my chin, guiding my eyes up. "Go fuck yourself, Zane."

"Okay," I said. "If you're into that, I can show you a few things."

She made a little choked noise, shaking her head in disbelief. Her eyes never left mine and it was still there, the raw and the rage, her jaw hardening like she was fighting the urge to literally bite my head off.

"Oh, for fuck's sake," she hissed. "Is that all you *ever* want? Seriously. What. The. *Fuck*."

Then she launched herself at me.

Maggie was a small woman, but it took me so off-guard, it brought me to my knees as she smashed her mouth to mine. I caught her in my arms, just barely, and her legs went around my hips as she kissed me with a fucking vengeance, all angry lips and teeth, her hands clawing at my neck, her fingernails digging in.

Holy mother of fuck.

Maggie was kissing me.

I gripped her tight and kissed her back like my life, my very next breath, depended on it, my heart slamming a fucking dent in the wall of my chest as my brain completely spun out. All I could think was, if I fucked her right here on the floor, would she hate me for it?

Because my gut was telling me to put her down... to let her go, to back the fuck off... that this wasn't right, that Maggie wasn't gonna be happy about this even *if* she started it... but my dick just wanted to make her scream and figure the rest out later, and my dick was a bull-headed prick.

I caught my teeth on her bottom lip and when she gave up a ragged gasp, my tongue plunged into her like a heat-seeking missile. I tasted her like I'd wanted to do for fucking years, desperate to have her, any way I could get her, angry, clawing at me, I didn't care.

Then it hit me, and I almost gagged.

The taste of liquor. Pungent and sour... revolting... and totally fucking intoxicating.

And I dove right into it.

I screwed my tongue into her mouth like I was tongue-fucking the neck of a bottle, sucking hard, the bliss of that taste and a brutal crush of memories smashing me in the back of the skull.

Then I caught myself. I almost gagged, again.

I ripped myself away with such force I shoved her off.

I spit out that bittersweet taste on the carpet and mashed the back of my hand to my mouth.

Yeah... not the best thing to do after kissing a woman. Kinda ranked right up there with laughing at her and throwing up.

I saw it in her gray eyes... the exact moment she started hating me. Or at least, hating me more than she already did.

Her face shut down and she wrapped her arms around her

chest as she sat there on the floor staring up at me, next-to-naked in her lace panties, looking small and so fucking vulnerable it gutted me.

"You're so full of shit," she whispered.

"Maggie—"

"Get out."

And for once, there was no arguing the point. I was the world's biggest asshole, and now she had proof.

I got the fuck out.

Chapter Three

Maggie

There were fuck ups, and then there were Fuck Ups. And I had just Fucked Up. Despite how I might look, given that I was on the petite side and my tastes ran to pretty makeup, manicures and four-inch-heels—in which I was still petite—I was a tough chick. Had to be, given the life I lived and the job I had to do. Which meant that Fucking Up the way I just did hurt in a way I didn't often feel hurt, because my night had already gone bad, I'd already been hurt bad, and now I'd taken that hurt from bad to worse.

And now I, Maggie Omura, the tough girl, the "on it" girl, the organized-as-fuck girl, the girl *always* armed with a plan, was at a loss for what to do about it.

For once, I had no plan.

I didn't even have the first clue.

Freshly showered and wrapped in a hotel bathrobe, I leaned against the low wall of the giant rooftop patio, gazing out over the shimmering lights of the Strip below, as if they might have answers. I had my sunglasses on, dimming the night around me, because my eyes felt suspiciously tingly and *no one* was gonna see me cry.

Not that anyone was around.

I'd already checked to make sure Coop and the groupies were gone; the main room of the suite was empty, the music turned off, and Zane was nowhere to be seen. The only thing out of place was a random lacy stocking, which I'd deposited in the trash before heading outside for some air.

The patio ran the full length of the penthouse, but I stuck to my own end. The last thing I needed was to wander past the glass doors that opened onto the master bedroom and glimpse Zane in there naked and doing God-knew-what.

I'd had enough of that man and his dick for one night.

You're just mad because he shoved you away before you got to the really good part.

Jesus, but you can be a perv, Mom.

God, why'd she have to butt into this? Not as if she'd never made any questionable decisions when it came to a charming, slutty rock star.

Guess this particular strain of masochism ran in the family.

I tore the foil from the top of the champagne bottle and untwisted the wire that secured the cork. To hell with my dad and his stupid free shit with all the strings attached. I was gonna drink his champagne, because fuck him.

And fuck Zane, too. Whatever his problem was, it was so not my problem. I just needed to remember that.

"Managing" the members of this band only went so fucking far.

I popped the cork and sucked off the gush of bubbly that erupted, hoping maybe I could lose the last hour-and-a-half of my life to champagne-induced bliss... because I couldn't even wrap my head around it.

I kissed Zane.

And he shoved me away.

Oh, and then there was that really fun part where he spat on the carpet.

Thank God for that, because it was just the punch in the face I needed. A reminder that throwing myself at Zane Traynor was a *complete and utter* Fuck Up.

I'd let him get under my skin, when I'd made it a policy, long ago, *never* to let that man anywhere near my skin. And now I was gonna pay for it in crazy.

Shit.

I got more than enough crazy from my dad.

I could not afford to let Zane's crazy overflow the professional bounds of our relationship just because I was hurt and angry—most of this hurt and anger misplaced, since it was my dad I was truly pissed at—not to mention horny, humiliated and vulnerable, and I lost my temper, snapped, and did something totally ridiculous.

It was my own fault, too. As much as I'd like to blame Zane, it wasn't exactly his fault I threw myself at him, no matter how big a dick he was being and how much that unfortunately, annoyingly messed with the signals between my clit and my brain. Acting on it—the anger and the messed up signals—was all me, and it was totally out of character.

Zane, for his part, was just being Zane.

Years ago, he and I had reached a kind of stalemate in our relationship. He wanted to sleep with me. I wasn't going to sleep with him. Neither one of us was about to budge, and as much as we butted heads over it, we kinda respected each other for it too. We were who we were, and that was just the way it was. He kept trying to get in my pants, because that's what Zane did. And I kept turning him down.

Simple. And the system worked for us.

Until it didn't.

Tonight the system totally crashed and burned. Thanks to me hurling myself, half-naked and angry, over that crucial line I'd never let *him* cross.

In the cold shower that followed, all I'd concluded about that was that for such a smart girl I could, on occasion, be really fucking stupid.

What the fuck was I thinking?

Like I was gonna teach Zane a lesson by shoving what he wanted in his face, once and for all? Like angry-kissing him for cockblocking my hookup was some kind of punishment?

And then what? What did I expect him to do?

Grope me, definitely.

Try to fuck me, probably.

And then I'd laugh in his face and shove *him* away?

Right. Really fucking mature.

More likely, at the rate I was going, I would've hate-fucked him into next Tuesday.

Great plan. Like that was gonna help anything.

Couldn't be any worse than being rejected by him, Maggie May.

Yeah, thanks, Mom. I kinda got that.

I flopped onto one of the cushioned lounge chairs and put my feet up, taking another few swigs straight from the champagne bottle. Yeah, so I was drinking alone and that was kind of pathetic. Plus, I was having a two-way chat with my dead mom in my head. Nothing new, but it might be a good idea to bring another living person into this for a sanity check.

I pulled my phone out of the robe pocket. There were a couple of work-related texts awaiting reply; nothing urgent, but I responded. Then I thumbed through my contacts. Under *Favorites* I had the members of the band—Zane, Jesse, Elle and Dylan—as well as my boss, Brody, our head of security, Jude… and yeah, my dad. Not that I ever called him. The only other person on the list was Jessa, Jesse's sister, my girlfriend who'd introduced me to the band and to Brody in the beginning.

I stared at the very short list, stunned.

How the hell had my personal life come down to this?

It was no big secret that over the years I'd grown apart from, drifted away from, or just plain alienated all my girlfriends back home. Not on purpose, but life with the band, on and off the road, and working twenty-four-seven had taken its toll. I couldn't remember the last time I'd had a meaningful conversation with anyone outside this fucked up little rock 'n' roll bubble I called a life.

Mom. But she'd died three years ago.

I might've called Jessa, but I knew she was in New York for work, which meant she was probably asleep right now. That, or getting laid. And I didn't really want to interrupt either of those activities.

Didn't really feel like hanging with anyone in the band, either. The way my luck was going tonight, far too good a chance of running into Coop, and I was not having that.

Zane was right about one thing. Coop was a pussy.

I was totally gonna burn his shirt along with my expensive hookup lingerie. I didn't need any souvenirs from the worst sexual disaster of my life. Rejected by two hot guys in the span of five minutes? Might've set a new land speed record on that one.

Way to go.

If my future sex life was gonna end up as barren as my list of friends, it wasn't looking good.

I tossed my useless phone aside and that's when it hit me, hard. I'd broken my own biggest rule by pouncing on Zane, who had all but vomited in response, and I had no one to talk to about it. No one to call up on a Friday night and vent to.

No one who loved me enough to snap me out of my funk and tell me I was better than this.

You are better than this.

Thanks, Mom.

I drank to that.

Then I heard a door open behind me and I cringed.

Please, please be anyone but Zane. The cleaning crew. Coop?

A half-naked groupie looking for her lost stocking?

No such luck.

Zane swaggered onto the patio, followed by room service. I refused to look at him, focusing instead on the giant room service tray the dude brought out and laid on the low table next to my lounge chair. It had a bowl of vanilla ice cream and a little glass pitcher of what had to be chocolate syrup, a stack of trashy magazines, and a martini glass filled with jellybeans—red, orange and purple only.

All my favorite shitty-mood fodder.

Zane tipped the room service guy and as soon as the guy was gone, he took the champagne bottle from my hand. His fingers brushed mine and I caught his scent, again... my guts clenching as the memory of our kiss slammed into me. I could still feel it. Could still *taste* it. And lucky me, I now knew Zane smelled almost as good as he tasted... like raw, clean man, pure sex and total fucking trouble. I could never quite put my finger on that crazy-delicious scent of his. A hint of cool steel and warm leather... and some kind of spice? Fresh ground cardamom and cloves?

Who the hell smelled that amazing all the time?

I watched as he crossed the patio and set the bottle on one of the weird pseudo-ancient-Greek-motif mosaic tables, out of my reach.

"Whoever decorated this place, it's tacky as shit," he muttered.

Yeah. It was.

I considered protesting about the champagne, but I'd already sank half the bottle anyway, and truth be told I didn't like drinking in front of Zane. Seemed kinda wrong. Like eating a giant piece of chocolate cake in front of someone on a diet... only so much worse.

Maybe if the person was deathly allergic to cocoa and one bite could end their life. Because that's what booze could do to Zane. I didn't even like seeing him touch the bottle, but shit, you had to have some faith in the man's ability not to self-destruct. Couldn't babysit him all the time.

God knew I'd tried.

I watched him pull up a chair on the other side of the table, an upright one, not a recliner like mine. He sat with his thighs spread wide, the top button of his jeans undone, and leaned way back. His leather vest was gone and he'd changed his T-shirt to a white one.

Guess I'd gotten "smarmy bass player" on the other one.

He'd showered, too. His hair was kinda damp, smoothed back from his face. It made him look harder and somehow more gorgeous than he usually did—which was really fucking gorgeous —as he looked at me with his ice-sharp blue eyes.

God, he was beautiful.

The man was born to be a star; anyone could see that.

But beauty aside, if Zane Traynor was shriveled and hunch-backed and covered in warts, I was pretty fucking sure he'd still find a way to get under my skin.

It was the king-of-cool way he spoke, the king-of-the-jungle way he took up space, the god's-gift-to-rock-'n'-roll way he sang; hell, the way he *breathed*; even the way his twisted mind worked... the way he looked at me like he'd eat me alive if I ever so much as gave him the chance, exactly like he was doing right now... yeah. The list of things about Zane that screwed with my mind and body on a moment-to-moment basis went ever on.

I never knew quite how he was gonna floor me next. I just knew he was going to.

Always.

I watched as he pulled a Zippo, a baggie of weed and a pack of rolling papers from his pocket and said, "You wanna tell me what's got your panties all in a twist?"

Yeah. Just like that.

King of cool.

The man just shoved me on the floor and then *spat* on that floor, all because I kissed him, and now I was the one with the problem. Made perfect sense, really, that level of crazy being just an average moment in the life of Zane Traynor.

Not so much in the life of me, and since my head was feeling a little fuzzy from all the champagne, I actually let myself *hope* I hadn't heard him right.

"*Excuse* me?"

"Dig in," he said, eyes narrowing as he flicked his chin at the ice cream. "Know a fellow junkie when I see one."

He wasn't wrong about that. I was definitely addicted to the sweet stuff, and no matter how ticked I was at him, there was no sense wasting good ice cream. So I dumped the warm, fudgy syrup over it and dove in while he fingered weed into the crease of one of the little papers. If this was a peace offering, it was incredibly effective. As the ice cream sank in, I could definitely admit I was more ticked at myself than I was at him. No matter how much his supreme coolness irritated me.

I watched as he ran the tip of his tongue along the edge of the paper and sealed up the joint. He sparked up the Zippo and lit it, then tucked the lighter away. He offered the joint to me, but I shook my head. Last thing I needed was anything else clouding my judgment tonight. Probably shouldn't have opened the champagne, but I didn't actually think I'd be seeing him again when I did.

He took a few short drags, exhaling a wisp of smoke as he studied me. Even though I rarely smoked it, I loved the smell of good grass. I didn't love it when Zane smoked up, though. Over time, I was afraid he'd just replace one addiction with another. I wasn't shy about voicing it, either. We'd debated it, ad nauseam, and it was Brody, not Zane, who'd finally convinced me to let it go. *Let the man have his weed. He's battled back a large-size demon, and you don't do that without earning some scars.*

That was some straight-up Brody-style man logic, but since he was usually right about anything and everything to do with the band and their business—professional and otherwise—not to mention he was the hands-down master of diffusing situations that were bound to otherwise end in me throttling Zane, I let it go.

Didn't mean I liked doing it.

Zane cocked his wicked eyebrow at me, the double-pierced one, as I watched him smoke. He took another slow drag, his eyes never leaving mine. "Your panties," he said, his blue eyes narrowing as he exhaled smoke. "They're all up in a fucking twist tonight, Maggs. Gonna tell me what that's about?"

My spoon froze halfway to my mouth, and it took a *lot* to get between me and ice cream.

I set my bowl down, my appetite leaving me, and tossed the spoon in so it clattered loudly. Then I drew in a breath, digging deep for the strength, the patience, and the will to resist committing murder that I was sensing this conversation was gonna take.

"I don't know, Zane. Maybe you could tell me why you've gotta crank the crazy on up to eleven. I mean, everyone knows you're pretty fucking crazy all on your own… but get you and me alone in a room together, and *Je-sus*."

He considered this a moment, looking completely unvexed. Then his gaze skimmed down to the gap in my robe where my thighs were on display, lingering a moment on my naked skin.

"Because I can't fucking think like a sane person when you're around and my dick is up."

Yeah. We'd kind of established that already.

But as much as I tried to pretend it didn't happen, my pussy clenched at his words.

Admittedly, it was a stupid pussy. Which was why it didn't call the shots.

Unlike Zane's dick, which definitely did.

"Nothing was gonna happen, Maggie," he added, as if reading my thoughts, his voice low, quiet. "You were hurting. I could see that."

Hurting? Yeah, I was hurting. But not so much about Coop, which was probably what he thought.

"Whatever you think of me and my track record with women, I'd never do you like that."

Well, that made me soften.

"I know that," I said.

I did kinda know. Was really nice to know it for sure, though.

"Anyway," he added, "I don't fuck women who've been drinking."

He looked so fucking serious I almost held back the laugh. "Right. Smoke pot much?"

"Totally different. Doesn't bother me the same."

"*Bother?*"

That's what we were calling it?

I'd seen the man drunk, pretty much constantly, for the first few months I knew him, and *bother* didn't even begin to touch the state he got into after a few.

"It's hard to explain," he said, breaking eye contact. "Temptation isn't the right word, but since I don't have a better one... booze and women together... that's a temptation I just can't hack."

Shit.

Shit.

My incredulous laughter died as I suddenly sobered. And now I felt even worse for jumping on him… and shoving my pickled tongue down his throat.

Okay, not like I was drunk or anything, but still.

It wasn't as if I knew when I drank that vodka that Zane was gonna show up and cockblock Coop, much less that I was gonna throw myself at him and attack his face. If I'd known that, I would've left the booze alone.

But *still*.

It was extremely impressive that Zane hadn't taken a drink in almost six years, especially when you considered the world in which he lived, and I was proud of him for that, but we both knew those six hard-fought years of sobriety could come screaming to an end with a single sip. Which was why I wasn't letting him off that easy, either.

"No? How about women who snort coke off the kitchen counter?"

He stared at me, unfazed. "I got rid of them, Maggie. What more do you want me to say? If I knew you were here, I wouldn't have brought them up." It was decent of him to say, and I knew he meant it.

And therein lay the most dangerous thing about Zane Traynor.

That being, that I was just masochistic enough to care about his ass, which made him and everything he did a threat to my well-being… especially when he looked at me like he was doing right now; like he cared about me, even more than he cared about getting laid. And Zane cared about getting laid a *lot*.

"Look, we can't have shit between us, Maggs. So let's just get this out." He took a final hit off his joint and mashed out the little roach in one of the big tacky planters shaped like a smiling sun. "Take your fucking sunglasses off."

I took them off, casually, like I'd been meaning to do it anyway. Actually, I'd forgotten I was wearing them.

It wasn't as dark out on the patio as I thought. The twinkly lights dangling along the walls really lit it up. It was kinda magical, really.

Romantic.

Too bad I wasn't gonna get to enjoy it like that.

"Didn't mean to push you away, Maggie," he said, his tone soft and sincere. "Really fucking sorry about that." He stared at me a long, long moment, unflinching, his cool blue eyes burning into mine. "You feel me on that?"

"Yeah, Zane," I said softly. "I feel you."

Maybe a little too much.

Chapter Four

Maggie

"So, you ever gonna tell me why we're shacking up tonight?"

Zane was still staring at me and I was staring right back, as he asked the one question I was really hoping he wouldn't ask.

Did he actually think I *wanted* to share this ridiculous hotel suite with him?

Yeah, not so much. Zane and I sharing a hotel suite could only end in disaster. Maybe I didn't picture him cockblocking my hookup and spitting on my floor, but Zane and I had never shared walls before. I'd always been really, really careful about that.

Because when Zane and I got alone in a room—which was not often—he got crazy and I got... weak. As in, my tough girl, smart girl self dove right out the window and my resistance to his diabolical charms got low.

Like dangerous low.

I'd just never let him glimpse how low before tonight.

And now the damage was done.

I'd kissed him, I'd lost my cool, and there was no taking it back. Really, all I could do now was try to salvage what was left of my dignity by making it clear I didn't *plan* for that to happen. It just wasn't gonna be easy or without any pain.

So I took a deep breath and accepted the fact that I wasn't getting out of this conversation. If Zane wanted to have it, we'd have it. Tonight, tomorrow, for the rest of the fucking year if that's how long it took for him to get it out of me.

Might as well rip off the bandage and begin the slow bleed.

"Because things got messed up," I started to explain, wondering how much I could edit out and still satisfy him. "We weren't supposed to share a suite. No one was. Except Jesse and Elle, but you know how that goes."

He grunted, and I knew he did.

"About two seconds after I saw you in the lobby, I ran into Elle," I said. "She looked upset, so I tried to help."

"Big fucking mistake."

"Yeah. But not exactly my job to walk away." Seriously. Elle had tears in her eyes when I'd seen her, and that was rare. "She said she and Jesse had a fight and we needed to get him his own room. Didn't really sound like a kiss-and-make-up situation. Which would've been fine, except the hotel's fully booked, so I couldn't even get us an extra room. The ones we have were booked months ago." Not that that was my problem, exactly. The tour coordinator usually handled such things, but since the rooms were booked through my dad, I insisted on handling it myself.

Last thing I needed was that man coming into unnecessary contact with anyone I worked with.

To that end, I'd given up my room to Jesse, so at least I was the only one out a room, and Jesse Fucking Mayes, hottest guitar player in the universe, wouldn't be slumming it on someone's couch—which he probably would without complaint, he was that cool, but no fucking way was I having *that*. So, problem half-solved.

Zane was shaking his head. "Those two aren't gonna last."

Yeah. I knew that. I saw it. Wasn't my place to say anything about it, though.

I wasn't close enough to Jesse, in that way, to say anything to him. Elle I could talk to, but when it came to shit within the band, I tread carefully. I wasn't in the band; she was. And I sure as hell wasn't in her relationship with Jesse.

Besides that... the woman was totally gone for that guy. She'd break herself to hell and back for him if she had to. I could understand, in a way. Jesse was gorgeous and talented; tall, dark and elusive. Elle was beautiful and talented, too. But Jesse wasn't the one who was head over heels in love; anyone could see that. He'd have to be the one to end it, and when he did, it would be bad.

I felt for Elle, but the band had to come first. That was the unspoken agreement we'd all made when we came on board this crazy train.

"What happens to the band when they don't last?" I asked, wishing I didn't have to. But this was the first time anyone had even talked to me about it. Brody and I hadn't even discussed it yet.

"Fuck all," Zane said. "They go to their separate corners a while, lick their wounds. And we keep doing what we do. Nothing's gonna break this band. Not ever. We'll be eighty and still doing our thing."

I cracked a smile, hoping he was right about that. Would be pretty interesting, to say the least, booking gigs for eighty-year-old rock stars.

"Think we could still get Coachella?" I asked.

He tipped his head back and gave a sexy laugh, and I tried to laugh with him. But his blue eyes were on me, and among his many talents—unfortunately, for me—Zane had the incredibly inconvenient talent of being able to read me better than anyone else I'd ever met. Including my mom, and I was *tight* with my mom.

Hence, why it was a terrible idea for the two of us to share walls.

"Give it up, Maggs," he said, his expression darkening as the laughter died.

"Give what up?"

"Maggie." He leveled me with his ice-blues. "Whatever it is you're trying not to say, but we both know you're gonna tell me eventually."

Right.

I cleared my throat, got brave, and let it bleed. "I talked to him tonight."

"Who?"

"My dad."

"Shit." Zane tensed like he'd been punched in the gut, pitching forward in his chair and leaning on his knees. "*Fuck.* I shoulda known. You should've told me, Maggs."

I shrugged.

Yeah, I should've known too. I should've known better than to drop my dad's name at the front desk when I was hoping to score an extra room. I'd considered just getting a room elsewhere, but I really didn't have the time if I wanted to hook up with Coop, and I totally did. Besides that, I needed to be close if anyone needed me. It nauseated me to do it, but I was desperate... as one of the owners of this tacky-ass hotel, he was my only hope. But I'd coughed that shit up for nothing. The hotel was still fully booked, and by the time the woman at the desk confirmed that with him via text, I heard his gravelly voice. I turned around to find a tall, blond, aging rock star standing behind me—my dad.

I'd hoped I could avoid him while we were in town, even though we were staying in his hotel.

No such fucking luck.

"What the fuck did he do this time?" Zane demanded, his voice going scary-low, stone cold murder flashing in his eyes as he read my face.

"Oh, you know," I said vaguely. "Dizzy has a way of making me feel extra special about myself."

"You really gotta stop talking to him."

"Yeah," I agreed, and I meant it. But I'd never do it. Totally cut off my dad.

He was my *dad*.

Even though he was a royal douche.

"I'm so gonna kill that dude one day," Zane muttered, almost to himself, as he flexed his fist and cracked his knuckles.

"I really wish you would."

He grinned at me, that heart-stopping, swoon-inducing grin, all beautiful, badass Viking with a side of cocky rock star, and I reached over and poked his knee.

"Seriously. Don't go all stabby on me, okay? I don't wanna have to explain that shit to Dolly."

Just what we all needed.

I'd already had to spring the man from jail enough times in my life. Not that he'd ever done anything *that* bad. No, Zane Traynor's rap sheet was a colorful list of minor offenses with descriptive words like "indecency," "disorderly" and "lewd." But the mention of his grandma, Dolly, the sweetest woman on Earth and the one who'd raised him after his parents checked out, made him soften.

"Okay." He settled back in his chair. "No violence. For now. Tell me what the world's greatest dad had to say."

Oh, *shit*.

Here I was complaining about my dad for being a douche, but at least my dad had been *somewhat* present in my life. Unlike Zane's, who'd been a raging alcoholic, ditched out on him when he was a toddler, and then gone ahead and died.

"Shit, Zane. Never mind. Let's just forget it. He's not worth talking about anyway."

"Maggie," he said, his eyes locked on mine with a casual air of command. "You can tell me what happened with your dad, or I can come over there and fuck you senseless, and then you can tell me what happened with your dad. Either way, you're telling me what happened with your dad."

Holy Jesus. Were those my options?

No. Definitely not the come-over-there-and-fuck-you thing.

"Fine. He insisted I have a drink with him and steered me into one of the lounges," I said, trying to pretend he didn't mean that little threat, because I was pretty fucking sure he did. "I figured I should just hurry up and get it over with, because—"

"Because you had a date with Coop," he said, his eyes frosting over.

"Well... yeah. But also," I added quickly, "because I didn't want to hang out and have cocktails with Dizzy. Every time we're in one room for too long, like over five minutes, you know how he gets. He starts talking about my mom, and how things should've been, and blah blah fucking blah, and I want to kill him."

Yeah, Zane knew. He'd heard all about the crazy stories my dad would weave, and his warped sense of reality. It was Zane who'd pointed out that after all the years of partying my dad had done, he might've actually believed the way he remembered things was the way they'd happened. Which was probably accurate, and about the craziest thing I'd ever heard.

But how do you get someone to own up to their part in a reality they never knew existed, because they were too wasted and self-absorbed to notice it happening in the first place?

"I never should've had that drink with him. I knew he wanted something. He gave us these hotel rooms for free, but no way they were really free, you know? Nothing with my dad ever is." That was a sad fact, because the man was insanely loaded. He just didn't like to share.

Zane nodded, taking this in. "So what did he want?"

"You," I said, forcing it out. "He wants to record a song with you."

Zane burst out laughing, that full-on, sexy-ass laugh that sent tingles down my spine... and if I dared to acknowledge it, straight to my clit.

"I'm fucking serious," I said.

"I know you are. That's why it's so fucking funny."

"*He's* serious. And it's not funny. He expects me to set up a meeting with you. He wants to do a full album, actually, but he thought you could start with a song. He's already written one and he wants you to lay down the vocals."

It was embarrassing to say it out loud, because it was pathetic. My dad had to know Zane would never do it; I was pretty sure that's why he was trying to go through me. To see if I had that kind of sway over the man—which had led to the ugliest part of our conversation... But my dad was so split with reality, I couldn't even guess what he really believed was gonna happen.

Did he actually think Zane Traynor, one of the hottest rock stars on the planet for the last decade, would want to record an album with his washed-up, one-hit wonder ass?

Possibly.

All I knew for sure was that Derek "Dizzy" Bowman was not a generous man, and he wasn't selfless either. There was no way he would've offered us free hotel suites while Dirty played Vegas if he didn't believe he could get something out of it.

I just hoped he didn't plan to accost Zane in an elevator.

"I can't believe he fucking asked you that," he said.

"Yeah." I could, absolutely.

This was exactly my dad. He only showed up in my life when he wanted something.

Last time, he wanted to talk to Brody about working with Dirty on a re-recording of his biggest hit song, "Schoolgirl." When I refused to set that up, I guess it pissed him off enough that he decided to try harder this time. He'd called Brody directly to offer the free rooms. Not like Dirty couldn't afford their own hotel rooms, but it was a luxury hotel and Brody had no real reason to turn down the offer. He also had no idea the extent of the shit I'd been through with my dad.

Not like Zane did.

I'd told Zane about Dizzy wanting the band to cover "Schoolgirl," and we'd had a laugh. Then he'd put his arm around me and held me close, and I'd so needed that at the time. *We'll never record that song*, he'd promised me. *I will never, ever sing that fucking song.*

I still didn't know if he knew how much that meant to me, but he did know I hated that song. And why.

My dad was thirty-one when he wrote and released that song, about a seventeen-year-old schoolgirl. Maybe not a big deal in itself, since adult male musicians had been writing songs about their infatuations with underage girls since pretty much the beginning of time. But in the case of my dad's song, the schoolgirl in question was a real person.

She was my mom.

And yes, she was underage when they met. She was seventeen when he knocked her up, yet somehow it was her fault they never rode off into the sunset together. Dizzy went on to become even more rich and famous than he was before he met her, thanks to that stupid song, while my mom raised me alone. My dad only ever paid the bare minimum of what he was made to pay in child support over the years, even though he was loaded, and now, after she'd died, he had the fucking balls to sit there and weave stories to me about how much he loved her and how they should've been together. Maybe he did love her, in his own warped way, but my mom never took Dizzy seriously. I never understood why she didn't get more upset about the way he ignored us, but I knew for a fact she never wanted to marry him.

"What did you tell him?" Zane asked.

"I told him I couldn't help him."

"And what did he say?"

"He said, 'You're management, you can steer him in the right direction.' I told him I don't make those kinds of decisions, or give that kind of career advice to Zane Fucking Traynor. But I did tell him you were pretty busy with Dirty and your other commitments."

Zane tipped his chin at me, a little proudly, I think. "Good for you, Maggs." He considered me sidelong, his head cocked in a dangerously sexy way that made my guts clench.

No, not my guts. A little lower than that.

"I gotta say, though," he added slowly, "even if you begged me, with my cock in your mouth, I don't think I'd ever record a song with that fuck."

"If I begged you with your cock in my mouth," I replied dryly, "I don't think you'd hear me."

His gaze held mine, something dark and twisted at work behind those ice-blues, but I refused to look away.

"Maggie," he said. "You know you deserve so much better than he ever did for you, right?"

"Well… yes," I said. And I did know it. Deep down.

Of course I did.

But holy hell, did I ever need someone to say that to me right now.

Okay. Not just someone. *Him.*

Hearing those words out of Zane's mouth and knowing he meant them made everything go kinda blurry around the edges. And as his gaze held mine, a familiar chaos began to unfurl inside me.

The thing about this was, I did not do chaos.

I did neat and orderly.

Zane Traynor was the last thing from neat and orderly, and I knew this. Zane Traynor was messy. Hence, why I did not do Zane Traynor.

Still, I'd tried my best over the years to keep our relationship neat and orderly. No matter how I tried that, my feelings for Zane were not neat and orderly; they were, in fact, a complete and total mess.

They were not rational.

They were complicated and, at times, utterly confusing.

Most of the time, they were not in my best interest.

Which was why I usually pretended they didn't exist.

What I'd learned from that? Denial was a powerful survival mechanism.

Until it wasn't.

"So how did you two leave things?" he asked, still studying me. "And don't tell me you ate more of Dizzy's shit, or I really will have to kill him."

I blinked at that, feeling kinda blindsided by this clusterfuck of emotion I had no idea what to do with.

One giant downside to being a tough girl who generally avoided getting the feels over every little thing? Kinda made it hard to process the feels when they showed up, and when they showed up large… yeah.

Cluster. *Fuck.*

But it was hard not to get the feels just now. Because, in a neat and orderly and even objective sort of way, the fact of the matter was that when Zane wasn't acting like a total madman and trying to get in my panties, and I wasn't avoiding him because I secretly wanted him in my panties but knew it was a very, very bad idea to let him go there, he was a great friend to me. Yes, Zane Traynor was without a doubt the most frustrating, perplexing, and maddening person I'd ever known.

He was also hilarious, patient, steadfast and smart, and he always had my back. He always nailed the one thing that truly mattered.

Zane was always there for me.

Always.

And I'd been there for him, too. At least, I'd tried like hell to be, no matter how many sleepless nights it cost me. I'd lied for him, against my better judgment, to countless women, covering for him so he didn't have to reject them in person. I'd picked him up, literally, when he fell down drunk. I'd bailed him out of jail when he got himself in trouble. I'd held Dolly's hand in the hospital waiting room when he got himself in worse trouble.

I'd been at the front of the line to kick his ass when he got out, too.

And if that was true, if we had that kind of friendship, I should be able to tell him everything, right?

All of it.

Right down to the honest and the ugly.

"Well... I, uh, told him politely yet firmly, again, that I couldn't help." I paused to clear my throat. I really didn't do so well with the heartfelt, emotional stuff, and this was getting dangerously close to a Hallmark moment. Time for a cold, hard bitch slap in the face, courtesy of my dad. "At which point he looked me in the eye and asked me what the hell I was managing for you guys if I wasn't actually managing your careers, which is when I told him he was out of line, and he told me I was a slut."

Zane's face hardened. "The fuck he did."

"He did. So then I told him he was a washed-up has-been with no real talent, and he told me I was nothing but a glorified groupie, of no more use to him than my mom, and I was a, quote, 'lousy fucking daughter.'"

Did I just say that out loud? God, it sounded so much worse coming out of my own mouth.

How could he say those things to me?

I mean, I'd said some harsh things too… but shit.

A whole world of crazy was going on behind Zane's blue eyes, and I looked away. It was more than I could handle just now, with my dad's words hanging between us. I felt utterly exposed, admitting all that shit to him. *My dad thinks I'm a loser and he hates me, and I have no idea why. I still fucking love his crazy, mean old ass.*

Life's a bitch, right?

I helped myself to some jellybeans, scooping up a handful and tossing several in my mouth. "Sweet family reunion, huh?"

It didn't end there, though.

Nope. My dad Dizzy was a class act. As I'd gotten up to leave, he'd tossed another pretty little nugget my way. He'd offered me his suite. The penthouse suite.

He'd been checked into it, but said he'd clear out, thus solving my room problem. It was two bedroom and two bath, and he'd take one of our single suites in exchange. So now we had the two bedrooms we needed, and all I needed to do was figure out who would room with Zane. Because Zane was the only one who'd bitch if he didn't get the penthouse… and everyone else would bitch if they had to room with Zane.

Hence, my ending up here, in this beautiful mess.

I'd ended up thanking my dad for it, hating myself for needing to thank him for anything, but I really needed the suite. And how did he top things off? By reminding me to tell Zane what we'd discussed.

If I call him cold and you haven't talked to him, how would that make me look?

Right. Because God forbid I did anything to make the infamous Dizzy Bowman look bad.

At that point, I'd gotten the hell out of there, collected Coop from the bar, and dragged him up here for a please-help-me-salvage-my-night fuck.

Good thing that turned out so well.

Might as well start laughing. I did that, and Zane just watched me lose it for a minute, his eyes narrowing.

"The fuck is so funny?"

"Nothing," I half-snorted. "Was just thinking how this night panned out exactly like I planned it."

"Right," he said. "You'd be in there getting drilled by Coop right now, that it?"

"Please," I said, popping another jellybean in my mouth. "Coop would never last this long."

Chapter Five

Zane

Jesus. How did Maggie put that smile on her face?

She was so fucking pretty when she laughed, it made the vise around my chest squeeze tighter at the thought of the shit that useless fuck of a father said to her.

"Babe," I said, "maybe you should slow down on the jellybeans." I watched as she shoveled a handful of them into her mouth. She seemed a little blitzed from the champagne, probably more than she realized. The sugar rush wasn't gonna help.

"It's okay," she said. "I'm not driving anywhere." Then she laughed, her soft, husky laugh, and I fucking melted.

Christ, but I was whipped for this girl.

I pushed the room service tray aside and moved to sit on the edge of the low table, facing her, leaning my elbows on my knees to look her straight in the eye.

"Don't punish yourself because your old man's an asshole," I told her. "You're better than that."

Her eyes locked on mine, and she sobered for a second. "Yeah," she said softly. Then she sat up, dropped the rest of the jellybeans back in the martini glass and stared at her hand. She sat there with her elbows on her knees, facing me, picking at the jellybean colors that had stained her palm. "You know if I don't laugh about it though, it just hurts?" She looked up at me with those gorgeous gray eyes, and I knew for fucking sure I could murder that man. Sleep like a baby afterward knowing he'd never hurt her again.

"I know, babe."

"He really, actually thinks I'm useless," she said, her voice wavering a little. "I swear he thinks you guys just keep me around as some kind of party favor. You know, like, 'Hey, I didn't have time to pick up some chicks tonight, here, just pass Maggie around.'" She shook her head and laughed, but there was no humor in it. "What an ass."

"Not your fault," I told her. "That's his fault, Maggs. His failing. Nothing you can do about it. Just how he views women."

Her eyes met mine, and there was a world of hurt in them. "Guess you would know," she whispered. She stared at me, and I stared right back. Then her gray eyes went wide. "I'm sorry," she breathed. "That came out all wrong…"

But we both knew it didn't.

"It's okay, Maggie," I said, my voice soft. "I'm gonna let you have that one, because you're right. I don't give a fuck about women. The only woman I've ever kissed and actually gave a shit about was you."

She stared at me, shaking her head a little. "That's pathetic."

"It is what it is. And you know why?"

"Why?" she asked warily.

I leaned toward her, like we were sharing a secret. A secret that meant fucking everything. "Because we're friends."

Her mouth curled in the whisper of a smile. "Yeah," she said. "We are."

"We are. And you know what else?"

"What else?" she asked, her tone still cautious.

"I think we should get married."

———

It took about five minutes for Maggie to stop laughing. I sat back in my seat, ate a few jellybeans, even flipped through one of her shitty magazines. Then I'd had enough. She was still laughing her ass off, sprawled back on her lounge chair, tears shining at the corners of her eyes. Clearly, she'd keep right on going if I let her.

I tossed the magazine on the table and stalked over.

"Oh, God, thanks," she said, wiping the tears from her eyes as I stood over her. "I really needed a good laugh."

I leaned down, set my hands on the arms of her chair, swung a leg over and lowered myself on top of her.

"What are you doing?" She started to jackknife up, but I was on her too fast. I got my knees on either side of her and dropped my hips to hers. She fell back against the cushion and lay staring up at me. The feel of her, soft and warm beneath me, delicate and strong, sent a rush of blood straight to my dick. I was already getting hard again. It was starting to piss me off.

"I'm asking you to marry me. You could take it fucking seriously."

And maybe I wasn't thinking straight, with all the blood hammering to my cock, but I never said shit I didn't mean.

Maggie knew that much.

I lowered myself down on my elbows, my chest to hers. I could feel her breathing, feel the swell of her tits, her nipples hardening against me through the plush robe as she squirmed.

"Okaaay," she said, like I'd gone stone cold crazy. "Do you have to do it right on top of me?"

"Yup. Got you to stop laughing. Looking good so far."

"What's looking good?" she asked cautiously.

"The odds you're gonna see the brilliance in this and say yes."

"Okay. Now you're kinda scaring me 'cause I think you're serious."

"I am serious."

She squirmed again, putting her hands on my chest and pushing lightly, like she was testing the likelihood of being able to push me off.

Not fucking likely at all.

I let my hips take more of my weight, looking for a comfy place to put my hard dick... like between her legs. Maggie's eyelashes fluttered as she struggled to hold my gaze. "Is this... ah... some crazy thing about getting in my pants?" she gasped out as I got comfortable.

"It's not about getting in your pants. We don't even have to have sex. We're just gonna get married. One thing at a time, babe."

She laughed, but the sound was forced. "Right. Because married people never have sex."

"I'm sure some don't."

"Get off, Zane." She shoved at my chest.

"Would love to," I told her. "Not getting up, though. Not until you say yes."

"To marrying you?" She laughed again. "Come on. What the hell kind of grass did you just smoke?"

"I think you're failing to see the genius in this plan."

She went still and her eyebrows pinched together. "What plan?"

Yeah. I knew the p-word would get her attention.

Maggie never could resist a good plan.

"The one where you marry me, tonight, in Vegas, and Dizzy shuts his fucking mouth and keeps it that way for the rest of his life."

She blinked, processing this. "Right. Until the second we get 'divorced' and he tells me he always knew it would happen because I'm nothing but a groupie slut."

"Fuck that. Who says we're getting divorced?"

She gaped at me. "You mean we wouldn't tell him?"

"We're not gonna tell him jack shit. Far as he knows, he came to witness our union and that's all the fuck he has to know. Beyond that, it's between a man and his wife. He's got a problem with you from that moment on, I've got a problem with him. He calls my wife a slut again and I break his face."

"Zane," she said softly, shaking her head. "That's not gonna work..."

"He never got married, never married your mom, right? So I marry you, he sees what I really think of you, he knocks off the disparaging comments, or I make him knock them off." I lay my hand on the side of her face, resting my thumb, lightly, on her soft bottom lip. "I fucking mean it, Maggs."

She shook her head, slowly, in disbelief. "You're fucking crazy."

"I'm a fucking great friend. And I'd make a great husband."

She laughed, hard, which cut me in a way I didn't care to acknowledge. "And how's that, do you imagine?"

"Let's see. I've got a great cock, I'm giving as fuck in bed, I'm loyal to a fucking fault, and I'd kill for you." Her expression got serious, quick. "Pretty sure I'd kill Dizzy if you asked me to. Pretty sure Jude would help me do it, no questions asked. Instead, I thought I'd marry you, which seems less complicated."

"It's really fucking complicated, Zane. If you think it's not, you've got no business asking me to do it. And where do you get off using the word 'loyal' when you go through women like toilet paper?"

"It's fucking simple, Maggie," I said, tugging gently on that juicy bottom lip with my thumb. "You're the one who always has to complicate things with your overthinking and shit. I told you, I've never given a fuck about another woman."

She rolled her eyes in extreme disbelief. "It's not that simple," she protested.

"It's simple as fuck. All you have to do is say yes."

She scoffed. "I say yes, and we get married? Tonight?"

"Tonight."

"Such bullshit. You don't even have a ring."

I ripped the big skull ring with devil horns off my index finger and shoved it on her thumb.

She rolled her eyes again. "An engagement ring, jackass. It usually has a sparkly thing called a diamond?" She pulled the ring off and stuck it back on my finger.

I locked on her gray eyes, daring her to look away or bullshit me. "I get a ring, you saying you'll marry me?"

"God... it sounds so fucking weird when you just say it like that..."

Yeah. I knew she was stalling. I could see her mind at work as she calculated the odds that I could find a diamond ring at this time of night, in Vegas... and then she got really scared.

"Weird or not," I said, "I'll marry you."

She stared at me, looking totally fucking bewildered. "Why would you wanna do that?" she whispered.

"To see the fucking look on Dizzy's face," I said.

Because I want you, I could have said. *Because I've always wanted you and I'd do fucking anything to have you.*

Probably should've said it, since it was true.

But she was still giving me that look that said she didn't trust my ass, and I didn't fucking like it.

It's not like I actually believed she didn't want me back. As much as Maggie pretended the fuck out of that being a fact, it was a bunch of bullshit. Straight up, I'd been with enough women to know when a woman was into me. *Deep* into me. Physically, at least.

More than that, I really couldn't say how deep things went between us. Not like we'd ever had a chance to explore it, since what Maggie wanted and what she was willing to do were two vastly fucking different things. I'd had six long, frustrating-as-fuck years to learn that much about the woman.

"We can't," she said.

"This is Vegas," I told her. "We sure as fuck can."

She just stared at me. We'd both gone still. My dick was still throbbing between us, her heart pounding against mine. But she wasn't shoving me away.

I wasn't getting up, either.

In my defense, it was *Maggie*.

Underneath me.

And she wasn't wearing any pants.

Shit like this didn't happen everyday. Shit like this *never* happened, actually.

Not too fucking sure why it was happening now, but as long as she was letting me get away with it, I wasn't gonna be the one to end it.

"If we do this," she said slowly, swallowing, "you can't tell anyone. It's just you and me and Dizzy. No one else."

"No one else."

"And you have to make the arrangements *yourself*." Her tone said there was no way in hell she thought I would.

"No problem."

"Right," she said.

Zero faith in me.

Jesus. When, exactly, had I fucked things up so royally with this girl?

No secret she'd been keeping my shit together for years, but that's because I *liked* her keeping my shit together. Didn't mean I was a fucking moron.

"I make the arrangements," I said carefully, slowly, so she couldn't pretend she'd misheard me. "We go do this. No excuses, no backing out. No Maggie May overthinking things bullshit. No blaming me if they don't have an Elvis impersonator available to officiate our shit or whatever. You say yes, you own it. You follow through with it. And I promise you, we'll make that prick of a father of yours eat his fucking words."

She narrowed her gray eyes at me, but I saw the sparkle in them. Tears. The idea of sticking it to Dizzy was just too sweet to resist.

And maybe it wasn't the best marriage proposal in the history of man, but it would have to fucking do. Not like I planned this shit.

Planning was for Maggie. I was more of a fly-by-the-seat-of-my-pants type of guy. Hadn't failed me yet. I was still alive. Plus, I had Maggie beneath me, her heart pounding against mine.

"Either that, or I kill him," I told her casually, running my thumb across her lip. "Your call, Maggie May."

"You don't have to kill him," she said, sniffing just a bit. "He's a douche but he doesn't deserve to die. I already lost my mom and my stepdad. I don't need to lose him, too."

Shit. That prick didn't come close to deserving this girl's love or forgiveness.

"Have it your way," I said. "But that's not a yes. I've gotta hear it from your lips."

She rolled her eyes. "Yes."

"Fucking finally."

I took my time getting up, re-arranging my throbbing dick in my jeans. Yeah... probably shouldn't have told her we could do this without sex.

Not sure what I was thinking on that one.

I looked down at her, lying there in her robe all askew. Her dark hair spread out around her face. Her wide gray eyes looking up at me, a little hazy from champagne... so fucking pretty.

I shook my head.

"Now get your ass up, woman, and go put on the best dress you've got."

———

Ten minutes later I had a car service booked and I was almost ready to go.

It took all of one phone call to the concierge to make the arrangements. So maybe I didn't do it *all* myself, but I didn't give them my name, just our room, which was in Maggie's name. If she didn't want me to tell anyone, I could do this shit incognito.

Felt a little strange not bringing my boys into it, though. Jesse, Jude and Brody had been like brothers to me since we were kids, and getting married was one of those things I would've thought they'd be here for, either to have my back, or to talk me out of it.

No fucking way I wanted to be talked out of this thing with Maggie, though.

If she couldn't talk me out of it, no one could.

I walked into the master bathroom, shaking my head. Maggie. Fucking ball-buster.

And that's when it really hit me.

Holy *fuck*. I was marrying Maggie.

Maggie was marrying *me*.

I stopped short as I felt that fucking *thing* overtake me, gripping me so tight I could barely breathe—my heart jackhammering like it did in that final moment just before I stepped onstage... when I always had a brief, private attack of self-doubt, never quite knowing how I'd be received.

Would they love me, or would they turn away?

I knew this was some screwed-up subconscious shit about my parents fucking off on me at such a young age. Also knew this was why, deep down, I wasn't good enough for a girl like Maggie. And maybe I'd never be. Because there was something wrong with me. Something missing.

Something gone, lost, that might never come back.

I started to sweat, just like I did in that moment backstage, the roar of the crowd loud in my ears.

How many times had I dreamed it?

Stepping out onto an empty stage, to find the venue empty, the sound of the crowd still thundering in my head and not a single person in the place. No one backstage, either. Even my band was gone. I was alone, but I could hear the concert rocking on the other side of some wall I could never get to.

The show had gone on without me.

Shit.

Just *shit.*

I splashed cold water on my face and just stood there leaning over the sink for a long, long minute, gripping the counter and letting the water drip down.

Did Maggie love me?

Would she?

I had no idea. No. Fucking. Clue.

I looked at myself in the mirror, right into my own eyes, and maybe it was wrong but I knew I didn't care. Didn't care at all what her reasons were for marrying me. As long as she did.

My eyelashes were wet, clumped together and dark, making my eyes look like ice. When I was a kid and I got over hating myself, I'd learned it was a good face. I'd never had a problem with women. Sometimes they had a problem with me...

Didn't care.

But Maggie? Maggie was different.

She'd always been different.

Ever since I met that girl, other women had been nothing but placeholders. Since that night, so many years ago now, when I cornered her and told her what I wanted... and she shot me down for the first time of many. Yeah. Just bed warmers, in the place of the one girl I really wanted.

And maybe I didn't plan to propose to her tonight, but it sure as fuck wasn't the first time I'd ever thought about making her mine. Far fucking from it. I just never figured out how to do it before—goddamn bane of my existence.

I dried off and took a giant, belly-deep breath.

Maggie.

Holy fucking shit.

What happened when you got everything you'd ever wanted? The one thing that truly mattered?

Did shit like that actually happen?

To someone like me?

No. Because she's not in love with you, asshole.

Fuck. Whatever.

Even if she was *only* marrying me because of Dizzy... by the time she woke up tomorrow, I'd make sure she knew she'd done the right thing. Hell, I'd spend the rest of my life convincing her of it.

Damn.

Motherfucking *Dizzy.*

I stood up tall and got my shit the fuck together.

My shoulders went back, my jaw hardened, I cracked my neck, and just like that, the adrenaline started building again. Just like it did as I forced myself to take the stage. To claim what was mine. To *make* it mine. My pulse took on the steady, solid thump of the bass drum, the don't-give-a-fuck self-assurance and the familiar confidence taking over.

No time for amateur hour stage fright bullshit. I had shit to take care of.

I'd found Maggie's phone on her patio chair and I used it to call her dad. Told him to be ready in ten. Just tried to keep the disgust out of my voice. Not easy. But the man was so eager to talk shop with me, pretty sure he didn't notice.

Head way too far up his own ass. Probably stoned, too.

How that loser made an angel like Maggie, I'd never know. Met her mom a few times though, so I could kinda see how it played out.

Maggie would be sad she wasn't here for this. We'd have to mention her during the ceremony.

I put on something marginally respectable, which meant a leather vest and jeans that weren't as ripped to shit as my other ones. I grabbed a cap to wear later; probably gonna need it. I thought about jacking off again, but I didn't do it. That one time in the shower would just have to get me through the next few hours. Easier said than done if Maggie turned up in a white dress anything half as slutty as what I'd been picturing her wearing ever since I proposed.

When I knocked on her bedroom door, it took her a few minutes to answer and the adrenaline buzz started to fade. She opened the door looking stunned, and not just a little bit confused.

No slutty white dress either.

"Holy ssshit," she slurred through her mouth guard. "You were fucking ssherioush." She had one of those blindfolds people wore to sleep pushed up on her hair, and silk jammies on.

Fucking hell.

"You were fucking sleeping?"

She pulled out the mouth guard, wiping slobber on the back of her hand. "Well, I—"

"Not cool, Maggie," I said, stalking past her into the room. "We had a deal."

I looked in the closet. Empty. Guess she didn't have time to go all neat freak on her clothes yet and hang them up in order of color. I dug through her travel case, ignoring her protests. I found some lingerie, hot pink lace, and tossed it at her. The closest I could find to a white dress was a baby-pink thing in a soft, clingy knit, which would totally fucking do.

When I turned to her she was holding the lingerie out with her fingertips like it was someone else's dirty laundry. "Zane, I can't get married in this!"

"Not my problem. You've had like twenty minutes to pick something out. We need a marriage license before we hit the chapel and the office closes in fifty minutes." I tossed the pink dress at her and she stared at me, still looking stunned. "Put this the fuck on and let's go."

Chapter Six

Maggie

"We're going *where*?"

I stared at Zane, my mouth gaping open. Pretty sure it was a super-hot look, combined with my bed-hair-and-pajamas ensemble. At the moment, I couldn't give one fuck.

"Wedding chapel," he said, playing with his phone, completely unconcerned with the fact that *we were going to a wedding chapel.* "Don't worry, Vegas is lousy with 'em."

When I just stood there, his blue eyes flicked up to meet mine, a spark of challenge in their icy depths. It was at that exact moment that the situation really slapped me in the face.

This was happening.

If anyone could pull off a stunt this insane, it was Zane.

The man had zero impulse control. I knew this. So why the hell was I surprised?

Yes, I told him I'd do this if he pulled it off. I just didn't think he'd actually do it, to the point that I'd brushed and flossed my teeth, put in earplugs and crawled into bed.

Basically, I figured once the high of acting on his impulse

started to fade and I was out of sight, out of mind, his ADHD would kick in and he'd be on to something else... like finding himself another orgy.

Apparently, I was wrong.

"Get the fuck moving," he said, a wicked-crazy gleam in his eyes I didn't even want to look directly at. What happened when you looked pure evil in the eye anyway?

Nothing good.

"Zane. We are not just going out and... and... getting *married*," I sputtered, "you know... without security." And yes, I was stalling. Desperately. The wheels in my head were turning way too fucking slowly. "I mean... I am not getting trampled in a stampede of drunk chicks on my... *Jesus*..." I stopped to swallow and work up the will to say it. "On my... *fucking wedding night*... you know, when they start recognizing you... and..."

I was starting to sweat. My silk pj's were sticking to my breasts. And leave it to my soon-to-be-husband—*holy shit,* that sounded weird—to notice it. His gaze raked down over my chest, zeroing in on my nipples, which pricked a little too eagerly at the attention.

I crossed my arms over my chest and looked at him pointedly. "Security, Zane. You take care of that little detail?"

"On it." He thumbed his phone and I tackled him. Because apparently jumping on Zane was now my thing. He didn't go down this time, though. He just stood there looking surprised and suspiciously turned on as I clung to him like a monkey, the phone I'd just ripped from his hand in my grasp.

I let go, dropping to my feet and backing away... the phone was already dialing Jude. Oh, no. No, no, no.

I hung up. "You are not calling Jude."

"You just said we need security," he said casually, studying my nipples through the silk pajama top again. Fuck it, let him look. I didn't have time to ward off his eyes and the full force of his crazy at once.

"Yes, and I told you when you 'proposed' that you can't tell anyone, and if you make Jude come with us, everyone in the universe will know by the time the sun comes up."

"Why'd you say 'proposed' like that?" he asked, and if I didn't know better I could've sworn I hurt his feelings. "It was a legit proposal, Maggs."

"A legit proposal usually climaxes with the presentation of a ring, Zane."

"Offered you a ring. And you ask me—"

"I didn't ask you."

"—a legit proposal climaxes with celebration sex."

And there it was.

"You *said* no sex."

He shrugged, like it was the world's most unimportant detail. "I said we didn't have to have sex. But let's stay on focus here, Maggie. Dizzy's waiting."

Right. Almost forgot about that ass, I was so busy dealing with the one in front of me.

At least the mention of my dad's name served to remind me why the hell we were even considering this crazy shit in the first place.

"Whatever," I said, shoving his phone into his washboard abs. "You're not calling Jude."

"Jude's discreet, Maggs," he said. "It's his job."

Great. We hadn't even gotten to the ceremony and we were already arguing. Again.

Ceremony... Jesus, that sounded official. Even though it would only be a *fake* ceremony, to screw with my dad... still. Jesus.

"Listen to me carefully," I said. "You can't tell Jude. Jude's best friend in the entire universe is Jesse, and he's going to tell

Jesse, even if we tell him not to. It's a given. You and me getting married tonight—even just for Dizzy's sake—is too juicy a tidbit to expect people to keep it to themselves. Do you get that? Jesse will tell Elle, and Elle is too close to Dylan not to tell him. Dylan will tell his best buddy, Ash. Ash is the Pusher's lead singer. Odds are he tells his buddies, too." Including Coop. Ugh. "Which means Pepper finds out, and Pepper will tell the whole fucking world." It was true. The Penny Pushers' drummer had a big fucking mouth. "Do you see the path of destruction?"

"Guess I can kinda see how that would go down," he said slowly, following my logic. "Pepper does have a big mouth."

"The biggest."

He eyeballed me thoughtfully. "You put that together quick."

"It's kinda my *job*," I said.

"So when you said we're not telling anyone... you meant literally anyone."

"That's right."

"For how long?"

"For-fucking-ever."

He stared me down for the longest few seconds in history, shaking his head like I'd truly fucking stumped him. Too bad. We were doing this my way—in secret—or not at all.

Finally he cracked a bemused smile. "You know, you're a strange one, Maggs."

"Trust me, my friend, you are way the fuck stranger."

He shrugged. Then he was back to his phone, all business. "I won't call Jude. We'll get someone else."

"But—"

"Trust me."

I bristled, and he caught it.

"If I'm gonna be your husband, you're gonna have to learn to trust me," he said.

"Don't start that shit."

"What shit?"

"Calling yourself my husband. There's still plenty of time for me to ditch your ass before we get to the altar."

He just smiled his crazy-hot Viking smile and stood there, staring at me, like he was waiting for me to go ahead and ditch.

Yeah. The bastard was calling my bluff.

I rolled my eyes. But I made no move to disappear.

"Go put that sexy dress on," he ordered, "or I'm marrying you in your jammies. You've got… six minutes."

I gave him my coolest, most unhurried look. "Sure. After you get out of my room."

"No problem. Meet you out there." He flicked his chin toward the main room and sauntered out.

I shut the bedroom door behind him. Then I tossed those slutty pink undies across the room in a frustrated snit and started digging through my travel case in search of something else. I wasn't sure what the right underwear to get married to Zane Traynor in was, but it wasn't those. If only I had some granny panties to put on. Serve him right if he tried to get up under my skirt. Knowing Zane though, it'd probably just turn him on.

Fucking perv.

I knew I'd found just the right panties and bra when I saw them, though. I grabbed my makeup bag and took everything into the bathroom to get ready.

I put on the lingerie, really fucking glad I'd had a hot date tonight—yeah, right—so I was all neatly shaved and moisturized. No marrying Zane with shin stubble. I pulled on the dress, made up my face with the basics—quick dash of mineral makeup, lip gloss and mascara—and smoothed out my hair, with a couple minutes to spare. With all the travel and the crazy pace of my work life, I'd become pro at doing this top speed, able to get ready for any given situation at a moment's notice.

Never thought I'd be doing it for my own wedding, though.

Probably would've thought I'd be paying a professional to do this when I got married. And maybe I'd have some friends here, getting ready with me?

Like who? Your good pal, Zane?

Fuck.

Whatever. This didn't really mean anything, right?

You'll get married for real, to someone kind and handsome and sane, when you're ready.

Thanks, Mom.

And by the way, you look beautiful.

For a moment as I stood back and looked at myself in the mirror, I felt proud and so intensely sad it nearly tore me open. I had to drop down to a crouch and take a few deep breaths to keep myself from crying.

God, she would've been so proud of me. Even like this. Even though it was a stupid pretend wedding and I was just doing it to stick it to my dad... she would've stood by me.

Hell, she would've laughed her ass off when I told her about it.

This isn't like you, Maggie May. But that's okay, too.

And she'd be right.

So I was about to do something dead-crazy and totally out of character tonight. This was Vegas.

Why not go all in?

So hitting up a wedding chapel with Zane Traynor wasn't exactly the least self-destructive thing a girl could do on a Friday night. It's not like I didn't know that.

In fact, I'd be the first girl to tell any other girl who cared to ask that Zane Traynor was exactly the kind of guy you screwed in the bathroom at some off-the-hook party after a few too many drinks; afterward, maybe you told your girlfriends about his otherworldly body, his giant dick and how many times he made you come with his demonic tongue. Maybe you masturbated to the memory a few times or a thousand. Then you moved on. You met that handsome, sane, regular guy who might also have an otherworldly body, if you were lucky, but who hadn't fucked half the continent.

Zane was *not* the guy you took home to your father, so to speak; even a father like mine.

He was most definitely not the guy you married.

No matter how much the idea might be sparking some misguided yearning deep in my gut, setting off a stupid thrill that was permeating my body and making me sweat just a little. No; Zane Traynor was *not* that guy.

Which was why I was not letting myself get carried away with what this wasn't.

This was not Zane suddenly doing a one-eighty and becoming the man of my dreams. As in, the hottest rock god I'd ever laid eyes on, talented, charming, *and* committed, suddenly willing to give up his legions of adoring groupies to throw down and love me—and only me—for the rest of his life.

This was Zane pulling a classic Zane stunt, and me, for the first time ever, going along for the ride. Willingly. A little recklessly, but with good reason.

And my dad was that reason.

Tomorrow we'd laugh about the whole thing and go on with our lives. Down the road, we'd have one hell of an inside joke. *Hey, remember that time we got pretend-married in Vegas to fuck with Dizzy?*

Hilarious.

I stood up, taking a few calming breaths. The tears still sparkled in my eyes but I blinked them back.

Not a real wedding. No crying allowed.

I checked myself in the mirror one last time for signs of distress. Nope. Shit totally together. And damn... the dress *was* sexy. Slinky, clingy and tiny, I usually wore it as more of a long shirt with leggings and a little jacket.

But when I stepped out of the bedroom a moment later and I saw the look Zane gave me, and the look Flynn gave me, too… I knew I could do it. I could rock this suddenly-a-bride thing.

"Flynn," I said, nodding my approval at Zane. "Good choice."

Flynn had been a member of Dirty's security team for three years, and he was solid as they came. And definitely discreet. The guy had barely spoken more than a few dozen words in my presence in the years I'd known him.

Zane grabbed a sweet little bouquet of pink flowers off the entranceway table.

"We're getting married," he said bluntly, answering the look of mild confusion on Flynn's face as he handed the bouquet to me.

I rolled my eyes. "*For now*," I muttered under my breath as I took the bouquet. The stems were cut short and it was tied with a white satin bow. It fit perfectly in my hand.

Nice touch.

Still, this whole thing felt hella ludicrous when I glimpsed the silent question in Flynn's eyes. I was pretty sure he wouldn't tell a soul what he'd seen, but I had to be certain.

I drew my shoulders back and held his gaze, undaunted by his size, the fact that he had a gun, or the cool, professional detachment that had settled over his features again. Yes, I was a small woman, but I ate rough-and-ready dudes for breakfast on a regular basis as part of my job. Security guys, roadies, rock stars… badass, manly men didn't faze me.

Just beautiful, batshit crazy ones, apparently.

"I swear on my mother's grave," I told him, "you tell anyone about this, I will kill you. You won't know where or when or how, but I'll do it. I don't care if you're all ex-military and shit. You will die. Slowly. I will kill you and all your future babies, too. You don't want to fuck with me."

"Know that, Maggie," Flynn said with a little nod. A small smile tugged at his lips as he looked down at me, all tough in my sexy pink dress and four-inch heels, holding my little bouquet of tulips.

Yeah, they were tulips. My favorite flowers.

I eyed my "groom" sidelong as he offered me an elbow. I took it, feeling kinda regretful for the thing about the babies. Over the top much? Whatever. Flynn didn't even have a girlfriend as far as I knew, much less any babies on the way.

"I love it when you threaten people," Zane said, and Flynn looked away, pretending not to hear. From here on in, he was just a fly on the wall... a blind and stone-deaf fly with a gun.

"Yeah," I said, a little sheepish. "I'm pretty good at it."

Chapter Seven

Zane

F lynn and I strolled into the wedding chapel to find a bridal party waiting in the small lobby and a ceremony going on in the main room, beyond a set of closed doors. I could hear voices and laughter. Hopefully they were almost done.

I walked right over to the small reception desk, locking on the woman who stood behind it.

"Hi," she said when she saw me, perking up. She was about forty, nice-looking in a MILF sort of way, her blouse buttoned a little too high. She looked friendly, though. Shouldn't be too hard to get what we needed.

"Hey, sweetheart." I'd put on my cap and pulled it low; no idea if she recognized me. "Looking to get married."

"Great," she said. "We'd be happy to accommodate you. It'll just be a bit of a wait. There's a ceremony in progress and another couple ahead of you. About... forty-five minutes?"

I leaned casually on the desk and looked her in the eye. "How about instead I give you whatever you make in a month, right now, to clear this place out and marry me and my girl."

She stared at me, a little speechless, but I could see the wheels turning. She glanced guiltily at the wedding party who were chattering excitedly on the other side of the room.

"Oh, yeah," I added, tapping the small glass display case next to the desk, "and I'm gonna need a couple of rings."

———

Minutes later, I walked back out to the limo, reached in and took Maggie by the hand.

"Who were all those people who just left, looking pissed?"

Damn. The girl didn't miss much.

"Don't forget your flowers," I told her as she scooted toward me.

"Got 'em!" Dizzy's date, behind her, held up the bouquet triumphantly.

Maggie scowled at me as she climbed out of the limo. I held onto her hand and steered her toward the chapel door. The woman from the reception desk was holding it open for us.

"I saw a woman in a bridal dress, Zane." Maggie craned her neck to see over the limo, where the wedding party I'd just had kicked out was piling into a couple of taxis. "She did not look like a happy newlywed."

I ushered her into the chapel, shrugging. "Must've called it off."

Maggie narrowed her eyes at me, but didn't call me on my shit.

Dizzy and his date, some ditzy-looking chick in a tube dress who could barely be out of her teens, followed us inside.

When we'd knocked on the door to his hotel room, both Dizzy and Maggie had been stunned when I'd formally asked him for his daughter's hand in marriage. He'd given his consent, looking way more astonished than I'd expected him to be. Apparently

Maggie was right that he didn't take her seriously, either as a member of Dirty's management team or as a woman I'd be fucking lucky to marry.

Just sealed it for me that we were doing the right thing. Maggie's old man needed to be put in his place.

Keeping my word to her, I'd made him promise not to tell a soul about the wedding until we said he could. Told him this was our night, Maggie's and mine, and we didn't need our relationship turning into a three-ring circus in the media. On that condition, we'd invited him to attend the wedding.

Pretty sure it would kill him to keep his mouth shut on this, but he'd do it for the honor of attending my wedding. And no mistake. The man was definitely more jacked about the fact that it was *my* wedding than his daughter's.

Such a prick.

He'd then produced this chick from somewhere in the shadows of his hotel room and insisted on bringing her along, and Maggie didn't seem to have it in her to refuse him. But as long as she kept her mouth shut, I didn't have a problem with it either.

We stood over to the side of the lobby as the double doors into the main room opened, and the wedding that had just finished cleared out. Maggie shook her head as she watched the staff usher out the bride and groom, a little too hastily. Then she leaned in and murmured in my ear, "You've got serious impulse management problems. You know that, right?"

"What I've got you for," I whispered back. I leaned down, nuzzling her neck and inhaling her sweet scent. "Managing all my impulses…" Then I reached around to grab a handful of her sweet ass and gave her tight cheek a slow squeeze for the first time ever.

I liked it. A lot.

She rolled her eyes but her cheeks flushed a little, and Maggie never fucking blushed.

I liked that, too.

The reception lady guided us over to the ring case and asked Maggie which wedding bands she wanted. Dizzy tried to butt in with his two cents, but Maggie wasn't interested.

"I just want to marry Zane," she announced sweetly, her arm wrapped around my waist, her other hand on my chest. "I don't care about the rings. Just pick whatever you like, sweetie." She fluttered her eyelashes up at me. I crossed my eyes and stuck my tongue out the side of my mouth. She giggled, which was totally un-Maggie. Maggie had a sexy, husky laugh.

She was really laying this shit on thick for her dad's sake.

Dizzy was either too wrapped up in his date or too clueless about his daughter to notice anyway. Probably both. But Maggie managed to steer him away, feeding his ego by asking for his input on a bunch of things I was pretty fucking sure she didn't give a shit about. Should his date be her maid of honor? Should we use the bouquet we'd brought, or use some of the flowers offered by the venue?

While they were distracted, I picked out some rings and took a look around.

It was a cheesy theme chapel, and the theme was rock 'n' roll. I'd gotten the recommendation from the hotel, but in keeping my word to take care of things myself, I hadn't let them call ahead for me. Was pretty sure I could make this happen with a little money. Didn't occur to me until the dude who was about to marry us asked me to sign a copy of a framed Dirty album on the wall that maybe the cash wasn't the only reason they'd let us take over the place.

I agreed to sign it on the condition that the staff understand this wedding was a private event, and they weren't to tell anyone about it. They agreed enthusiastically, especially when I beefed up their tip. Then I scribbled Dylan's signature on the album instead of mine, grinning to myself. My drummer's autograph was totally fucking illegible. Pretty sure they didn't know it wasn't mine. If it was, no one would believe it was mine anyway.

I was the last guy in the band anyone would ever expect to find hanging out in a wedding chapel. Which was saying a lot. My band brothers weren't exactly famous for their long-term relationships.

Then again, no one had ever seen me with Maggie.

Not like this.

Even I didn't know what it would be like. What it would feel like to actually be *with* her. But I found my eyes following her around the chapel as she and Dizzy looked around, and it felt fucking *good.*

Sure, this had started out on a whim. At least, the proposal part. A testosterone-fueled impulse, brought on by Dizzy's shitty treatment of his daughter and my own gut-deep urge to do anything in my power to protect her from him.

But it was an impulse six years in the making.

The fuse had been lit the day I met Maggie, and I'd been burning for her for a long, long time.

The closer we got to walking down that aisle? I was warming more and more to the idea of making her my wife.

Despite what my friends might think, what Maggie might think, I could totally do a wife and a marriage. If it was Maggie. Why the fuck not?

I'd had every kind of fantasy there was about the girl, and seeing her in that clingy pink dress holding those flowers? Yeah, I could be all over that.

My wife.

"So… what are you doing later?"

I glanced down to find Dizzy's date getting up close and personal.

"You know," she added, "after this?"

I stared at her. *The fuck?*

"I'm boning my new wife," I told her, deadpan.

She smiled a little, and that's when I noticed her eyes. She was blitzed on something. Didn't smell of booze, though.

"Oh yeah," she said, kinda dreamily. "She's so pretty." Then her thoughts seemed to wander away, and so did she.

I shook my head.

"We're in luck, sweetheart," I heard Dizzy say. "They've got my song." I turned to find Maggie's dad stuffing coins into a jukebox and looking over at Maggie.

Sweetheart?

Guess he was pretty fucking pleased with this whole event, then. Big improvement over calling her a slut.

Then the song kicked in and I cringed.

"Schoolgirl."

Christ, but the man was clueless.

My gaze slammed into Maggie's across the room. Her face was turning pink to match her dress. I couldn't tell if it was repressed rage or laughter, or maybe some kind of allergic reaction to the song. Whatever it was, she bit it back and smiled, the epitome of the happy, blushing bride.

"Perfect!" she said cheerily.

She steered Dizzy and his date over to talk to the officiant, then came over to me while Dizzy pummeled the guy with questions, rolling her eyes. I actually felt kinda sorry for the guy, but dude was in the wedding business. Couldn't be the first time he'd had to deal with an asshole father of the bride.

"Hey," I said, taking her hand and drawing her close.

"Hey." She looked up at me and bit her lip. And yeah, I liked fighting with Maggie, but even better than fighting with Maggie was seeing that truly rare but fucking beautiful spark of mischief in her eyes, the one that said we were on the same team. "I wanted to tell you... I was never that girl who dreamed of some big traditional wedding, you know?"

"That's good, because this place is a fucking dive."

She glanced around and shrugged. "Yeah. Good thing it doesn't matter. But sometimes traditions can be nice. And since this whole thing is hella unconventional..." She grinned. "You know that 'Something old, something new, something borrowed, something blue' thing?"

"Sure."

"Well..." She glanced over her shoulder to make sure Dizzy was out of earshot and leaned into me. "Dizzy's the something old," she whispered.

I laughed. "Perfect."

"And the flowers are new," she said, twirling her bouquet. "Something borrowed... I thought maybe you could lend me that skull ring?"

"It's yours." I took it off and slid it onto her thumb again. Her thumb looked tiny and delicate engulfed in the big hunk of silver.

"And... well..." She reached down. "I know you picked the pink ones, but I needed something blue." She slid the dress up her thigh and flashed me the electric-blue lace of her panties.

Instant flood of lust, straight to my dick.

"I think, traditionally, it's supposed to be a blue garter, but I didn't have one of those on short notice." She bit her lip again, smiling. "You think this'll work?"

"Yeah," I said as she lowered her dress back down. "It works, babe."

Then I leaned in and caught her mouth with mine. Just felt like the right thing to do.

I was *marrying* the girl.

I wrapped my hand around the back of her head and kissed her slow. I held her tight, breathing with her. I didn't want to let her go. I just wanted to taste her, to smell her, to make her mine in every way.

Should that have scared me?

Maybe.

I'd never wanted anyone like this. Never wanted anyone to belong to me.

Never wanted to belong to anyone... until I met Maggie.

She pulled away, licking her lip and gazing up at me, heat and a strange unease thudding between us. Couldn't say what it was. Didn't know if it was bad or good. Just knew I wanted to kiss her again.

I leaned in and brushed my lips to hers.

"Hey, you two."

Dizzy's voice grated through the moment and I felt Maggie stiffen.

I glanced over at him. He was standing by the open doors into the main room, at the foot of the short, red-carpeted aisle, and wearing a shit-eating grin. He offered an elbow to Maggie, and I walked her over, gently handing her off to him.

"Let's do this," he said, and Maggie smiled.

———

"I've got something to say."

The ceremony was short and sweet, but when the dude launched into the standard wedding vows bullshit, I spoke up, cutting him off.

"Oh... I'm sorry." He looked from me to Maggie and back. "It was my understanding that you hadn't written any vows."

"We didn't," I said, holding Maggie's gaze. She looked a little panicked. Probably wanted me to just stick to the script, but fuck it. "Got something to say to my bride."

The dude cleared his throat and gestured for me to take the floor. "Of course."

"It's not much. Just something I need to say to you, here and now, in front of your dad." I didn't even glance over at Dizzy.

Didn't have to, to know he was eating this up. "The first time I met you," I told her, holding her hands tight in mine and looking straight into those gray eyes, "I thought you were adorable. Also thought you wouldn't last. You had those invisible braces, remember?" She smiled a little and chewed on her lip. "And so much fucking courage. You stayed. You never gave up on me, even when you should've. Since the beginning, you've been my girl. Even though you didn't know it yet. Far as I'm concerned, this is just making official what I've always known. I love everything about you, Maggs, even the stuff that annoys the shit out of me, and I'm never letting you go."

Her gray eyes flared at that. Probably because me declaring outright in front of Dizzy that I was in this for the long haul went against her little plan that we'd soon get "divorced." Well, fuck that. She agreed to marry me.

I never agreed to give her a divorce afterward.

She stared at me, stammering out some stuff about loving me too, when the dude prompted her.

After that, I'd have to say it was kind of a blur. Maybe because my eyes were kinda wet.

Chapter Eight

Maggie

"You catch the look on Dizzy's face when they pronounced us husband and wife?" Zane nuzzled into me so he wouldn't be overheard; his arm went around my waist. He'd barely let go of me since we'd left the hotel.

To any observer, we probably looked exactly like newlyweds should look. Happy, a little adrenalin-buzzed, and all over each other. Random people honked their horns at us as they drove by.

We were standing on the curb outside the chapel, about to pile back into the limo, and Zane had put his cap back on, so I didn't think anyone saw his face. They were just happy for us. Total strangers, and they were probably happier for me than my own dad was.

Dizzy was happy, sure. For himself.

I sighed, because yes, I'd seen the look. Not a look I could recall ever seeing on my dad's face. Pretty sure it was pride.

Lukewarm approval was about the closest I'd ever seen before, and that was years ago, when I'd first told him I'd been hired to work for Dirty. At the time, he'd been a lot less interested in the particulars of my job than in what name I'd be using for work; he was royally pissed when I told him I'd be continuing to use my stepdad's last name, Omura, instead of his. Dizzy was adamant that having his last name would open doors for me in the industry, but I wasn't *that* naive. I knew he was more interested in what doors might open for *him* if he could associate himself in any way with Dirty.

For a moment, I allowed myself to wonder what he'd think when he found out I wasn't taking Zane's last name either. He'd probably say that was a mistake, too. Good thing I didn't care what he thought, right?

Except that I did care. Hence this whole ridiculous farce.

Yeah, I really had to do something about this fucked-up little masochistic streak of mine. Starting tomorrow.

"I saw it," I murmured distractedly, as we watched my dad making a flashy, embarrassing spectacle of tipping the chapel staff.

"Should we rescue them or what?" Zane asked, flicking his chin at the staff. They'd been pretty much trapped by Dizzy, who was waving a fistful of cash around as he told them some bullshit story about whatever great thing he figured he'd done most recently. Dizzy had a bullshit story for every occasion. Especially when he'd been using.

"No," I said, but I appreciated Zane deferring to me on this. No one could really "handle" my dad, but after the years I'd spent working with Dirty, I had a knack for knowing when to step back and let the biggest ego in the room have the floor. "Just let him have his moment."

For fuck's sake, though. You'd think *he* was the one who'd just gotten married. I just hoped he wasn't being rude.

The chapel staff had been incredibly accommodating, and my suspicion that Zane had paid them to shut down for us had been confirmed—by my dad, at his first opportunity. It was grotesquely clear to me by now that in his eyes, the fact that I'd just married a man who had the cash, the influence, and the balls to do that kind of thing meant I'd won the husband lottery. In fact, he'd warmed up extremely fast to the idea that I was marrying someone who, in his mind, was a lot like him. This, evidenced by the fact that he'd used the phrase "Zane and I..." to start about every second sentence he'd uttered since we left the hotel.

As in, *Zane and I would've preferred you in a white dress, Maggie.*

And so on.

Which just got me thinking...

I eyed my dad and tried as hard as I could to see him objectively.

The frizzy, bleached-out hair, all scraggly and black at the roots. The grossly tight jeans. The studded boots, the many necklaces and the earrings. The sleeveless Harley-Davidson shirt that showed his overly-tanned arms, now the texture of jerky; the tattoo of a voluptuous girl busting out of a bikini on his right bicep.

It all used to look so badass when he was younger. I could remember thinking he was just so cool. He'd flitted in and out of my life, and he always had some magical excuse for it. He was like a superhero to me then.

But now I was grown-up, and Dizzy was just ridiculous.

This was an extremely wealthy man who'd never treated his own daughter with much respect, forget about genuine affection or love. And now he was alone, clinging so desperately to his stoned-out youth that he was screwing chicks who were younger than his daughter and probably had daddy issues of their own.

I just hoped this one was legal.

Shit.

Was Zane gonna end up just like my dad in thirty years?

Didn't matter, I realized. I wasn't going to be married to him that long.

I wasn't going to be married to him at all.

Sure, I'd said my vows and signed the papers and went through the motions. I'd "married" Zane in a super tacky all-night wedding chapel in Las Vegas, in front of my dad and some girl named Maxxi. Yeah, that's with two x's. She spelled it for me.

It couldn't have been any more ridiculous, but apparently Dizzy had bought it. Big time.

Other than Zane being pretty sweet about the whole thing, it was kind of humiliating. I just couldn't decide if it was more humiliating for me or for my dad.

Zane's hand dropped to my ass and he gave my cheek a squeeze. He'd done that about ten times since we'd arrived. I didn't mind. It was pathetic to me, and incredibly hurtful, that my dad thought more of the man I was marrying than he did of me, and his comments in the hotel bar tonight still stung. If this was what it took for him to finally dredge up a modicum of respect for me, then so be it. I wanted him to see my new husband all over me, and for his part, Zane was taking every advantage of the opportunity.

"Get your sweet ass in the limo, wife," he said, his smoky voice all kinds of suggestive. Then he nipped my neck with his teeth. "It's time to celebrate."

"We are not celebrating," I said coolly, trying to stave off the shiver that pricked its way down my spine. Zane's idea of "celebrating" was bound to involve his dick in my pussy, and despite the fact that I'd been glued to his side for the last hour, I was not down with that.

I was way too sober—not to mention sane—to be down with that.

"Fucking right, we are," he murmured, and this time he nibbled on my ear, just scraping his teeth lightly over the curve of the lobe. And damn, I couldn't keep still. I squirmed a little as I shivered again, pretending to be cold as I burrowed deeper into his arms.

"No," I said into his shirt. I was putting my foot down on this. No fucking way were we "celebrating" this craziness. I just wanted this whole thing over with.

"C'mon, Maggie." Zane gripped my head and tilted my face up. "We just got married and I wanna go shake it up before you pop my cherry," he whispered, his lips hovering so close they brushed against mine. "Don't worry, we'll keep it low-key."

Right. Low-key.

And popping his cherry? Pretty sure some other woman had that honor, many, many years ago... his high school music teacher, if I remembered the story correctly.

No one was popping anything tonight, except maybe a couple of Advil before passing out.

"No, Zane," I whispered back, my voice firm. "Let's just go back to the hotel." I only heard how it sounded once the words were out.

Zane didn't miss it.

"Straight to bed, huh?" He cocked his pierced eyebrow at me, stroking my cheek with his thumb. "That's cool. We can do that instead, if you'd rather—"

"Forget it," I cut him off, untangling myself from his arms. "Let's go shake it," I announced, loudly enough for everyone to hear, as my dad and his date headed over to us.

Maxxi whooped excitedly. My dad smacked her ass and I followed them into the limo, tugging Zane along behind me as Flynn brought up the rear.

Dizzy was already opening a bottle of champagne that he'd produced from somewhere as I settled into my seat with a sigh... and pasted on my most dazzling newlywed smile.

So much for putting my foot down.

———

When we arrived back at the hotel almost four hours later, my head was still ringing from the music in the all-night karaoke bar that was the last stop on our whirlwind tour of late-night Vegas. It was Zane who'd insisted on the karaoke. He'd been going on about popping cherries again while we perused the song selection, and when I realized he was planning to serenade me, I'd hissed at him, "Don't you dare sing 'White Wedding'!"

Then my dad piped up, telling Zane with a heavy slur that he should sing "Dirty Like Us," and I wasn't even sure if it was an actual mistake that he got the name of Dirty's most famous song wrong, or if he was just being an asshole getting it wrong on purpose, but neither Zane nor I bothered to correct him. I did slap my hand down over the Dirty songs on offer though, including "Dirty Like Me," since it would give him away in a dead second if Zane decided to saunter on stage and start singing that panty-wetting, now-classic rock anthem of love, hate, and soul-sucking heartbreak. "And no Dirty!" I ordered.

Instead, my wiseass "husband" chose another Billy Idol classic, "Rebel Yell." Which he sang arguably better than Mr. Idol himself, and holy fucking shit, who knew that song was so sexy? His performance, with ball cap pulled low over his eyes, raised so many eyebrows, we just barely scraped our way out of there before he lost his pants.

Flynn was sweating when we piled back into the limo.

In front of the hotel, I was wobbling a little on the curb as everyone piled back out. I gave Zane a serious once-over, and my most managerial stare down. "That was the sexiest karaoke, ever. And karaoke is never sexy. So you do the math on that."

He pulled me close and steered me into the hotel. "You're drunk," he whispered in my ear, his hot breath on my neck making me shiver.

"Am not."

I kinda was.

We said good night to Dizzy and Maxxi. They were wasted and my dad hardly noticed our departure. At least he'd stayed coherent enough to witness the wedding; that was all that really mattered.

Still... would it have killed him to offer a half-hearted "Congratulations" or a hug or something?

Apparently.

He was too busy pawing Miss Barely Legal to even say goodbye.

As Flynn dropped us at our door, I convinced myself it was all for the best. No point drawing this out. It was done, and now I could leave my dad hanging as long as I wanted to. For all he knew, I could spend the rest of my life happily married to Zane, a man he obviously admired. A lot. It's not like he'd notice we weren't actually together. My dad and I didn't live in the same city. Christ; Zane and I didn't even live in the same city. I still lived in Vancouver, where I'd grown up and where Brody also still lived. Zane lived down in L.A. most of the time.

Dizzy now lived in Vegas.

Yeah. He'd never know. Not if we didn't tell him.

He'd never been the world's most observant father.

When Zane and I walked into the penthouse suite, that fact was made abundantly clear. Not only had Dizzy bought into our little charade, he'd bought into it so hard, it had inspired him to do something totally out of character. Something thoughtful.

He'd put his staff to work for us, big time.

The big double doors leading into the master bedroom stood open. Red and white rose petals had been scattered along the floor, leading a trail up the three stairs into the room and straight to the massive bed. The bed had been covered with a fluffy white duvet, turned down to reveal white satin sheets. Giant bouquets of exotic flowers burst from vases set atop every available surface. There was a fruit tray and chocolate truffles and fresh oysters on ice. And a card, which I opened. It was signed in a hand that wasn't my dad's.

With my deepest blessings. Dizzy.

What a fucking tool. Like I gave two shits about his blessings. I passed the card to Zane. He scanned it and tossed it aside.

Dizzy had never done anything like this for me before. Not when I graduated high school or college, not when Dirty hired me, not when I bought my first home. Nothing I'd ever done had warranted more than an absent "Good for you, sweetheart" when we'd spoken over the phone. Which was how I knew this had exactly zero to do with me.

This little display was for Zane.

Correction; actually, it was for Dizzy himself. To make him look like father of the year in the eyes of my new rock star husband.

Good luck with that, Dad.

Oh, and there was more champagne. Because that's just what I needed; more booze.

I stumbled a little as Zane let me go. He'd kept his arm around my waist all the way up to the room, and he eyed me warily as I got my footing. Whatever. My high heels were *high*. Yes, I'd had a bit to drink while we were out. Maybe a bit too much. But who could blame me? I'd just gotten pretend-married on a moment's notice to Zane in front of my dad, who thought it was real.

Obviously I understood why Zane was going dry, but I wasn't the one with the drinking problem. So why should I suffer through a night with Dizzy sober?

In the limo, it was Zane himself who'd handed me a flute of bubbly. I had no idea if my dad had a clue that Zane didn't drink. Zane just passed politely on the liquor, and no one seemed to care.

Zane didn't bat an eye as I sipped the champagne, and honestly... maybe I did it to force some distance between us.

He said he didn't do chicks who'd been drinking. What better way to ensure he wouldn't try to feel me up when we got back to the hotel than getting a little buzz on?

I watched him take off his vest and kick off his boots. I still had the bouquet of tulips he'd given me, which had miraculously survived our bar-hopping. I went to put the flowers in a jug of water in the kitchen, avoiding his eyes, and told myself not to feel guilty for being a little inebriated.

This wasn't *actually* our wedding night.

Yes, it felt weird drinking in front of Zane. At least, for the first couple of drinks. But we were in and out of so many bars tonight and people were indulging all around us. What difference could it make if I had a few?

It was Zane who'd convinced me to do body shots off a waitress. That was at the strip club Dizzy decided we should hit. It was also Zane who bought me a lap dance. From a chick, which wasn't exactly my thing. She took us into one of the private rooms and I endured it for about a minute, because it made Zane laugh. But then I decided it would be a hell of a lot more fun making her sit in the chair and teach me some moves. And damn, did I ever work my tiny pink dress.

At least, it was fun until I remembered my dad was on the other side of that same room.

Luckily he was making out with Maxxi at the time, so he missed my little performance. Zane, on the other hand, didn't miss a thing. He even tipped me afterward. Also kinda fun.

But standing there in a private room in some strip club with my dad while Zane stuffed cash into my lace panties, I decided it was well past time to call it a night. This night was already fucking weird enough. Didn't think I could handle it getting any weirder.

I'd spent the ride back to the hotel quietly sipping a bottle of water and wondering why I'd let myself drink so much.

Maybe I'd been more nervous about this whole crazy thing than I'd let on... even to myself.

Still, I'd somehow managed to rationalize the booze, just like everything else, as harmless enough fun—until I stepped back out of the kitchen with my bouquet and looked up to see the weird-ass expression on Zane's face.

We stood there, awkwardly, on opposite sides of the room, staring in at the giant bed all decked out for a night of matrimonial bliss.

"If you want the big bed with the satin sheets you can take it," he said. He'd turned to look at me, and I could not for the life of me read the look in his blue eyes. "I'll take the other one. Whatever you want."

I blinked at him and set the flowers on a table, wobbling a little in my high heels. Whatever *I* wanted?

What the fuck?

"We aren't sleeping together?"

The words came spilling out of my mouth before I could think them through.

Zane's eyes twitched like he might smile, but then he didn't.

"I'm gonna go wash up. Take whichever bed you want and I'll take the other one. Cool?"

I stared at him, totally speechless.

No.

Not cool.

Maybe he was ready to call it a night—why??—but I'd spent the better part of the last four hours, pretty much from the second we said "I do" and he kissed me like he was devouring a bottle of particularly expensive bourbon, mentally preparing myself to spend the rest of the night, from the moment we walked back in here, fending him off.

Well, that, or fucking his brains out. If I was being honest. Hadn't quite decided which way things were gonna go yet. Blamed the champagne for that. Definitely.

But this? This was bullshit.

I watched him stroll up the stairs, through the master bedroom to the en suite bathroom, turn up the lights, and disappear inside. He closed the door behind himself. Not all the way, but still. A civilized person knew what a closed bathroom door meant.

But fuck that.

I heard the water running in the sink as I approached, and tossed the door open to find him brushing his teeth. I stalked over and turned off the faucet.

"This is my wedding night," I told him icily. "You have to at least *try* to bang me, so I can turn you down."

He pointed at the sink, which I was standing in front of. Never mind that there was another one two feet over.

I crossed my arms, staring him down.

He pulled the toothbrush out of his mouth. "May I shpit?" he asked, his mouth full of toothpaste foam.

"Fine." I shoved away from the sink to let him at it. Then I grumbled, "Like you didn't do enough of that already tonight," as he spat and rinsed.

"And like I told you," he said, eying me as he dabbed his mouth with a towel. "I don't fuck chicks who've been drinking."

"I'm not even drunk!"

He gave me a level look. "Babe."

"I'm not!" Pretty sure I was. Didn't keep me from protesting the fact. Hard. "Look, I'll brush my teeth. You won't taste a thing." With that, I seized his toothbrush and brushed my teeth.

He stood back, watching.

"See?" I spat in the sink and rinsed, then gave him a winning smile. "Minty fresh."

"You used my toothbrush," he said, eying me with mock concern. "You know that has cooties on it, right?"

I rolled my eyes. "I'm your *wife*," I shot back as sarcastically as possible. "I can't use your toothbrush?"

I strutted back out into the bedroom, still trying to prove my case. Zane followed at a distance. I wasn't sure why it was so important to me that I prove I wasn't wasted. In the bar it really hadn't seemed like a big deal, especially when he kept feeding me drinks.

Now it felt wrong.

"What do you want me to do? Walk a straight line? Touch my finger to my nose?" I did that, and thank God I actually hit the target. "What if I sing 'Schoolgirl'? Bet I can remember all the words."

Then I started singing my dad's shitty song. Not terribly, either. I could hold a tune. Couldn't hold a candle to Zane's voice, but at least I wouldn't totally embarrass myself. The booze loosened me up, so I figured I sounded even better than usual. Though my judgment was probably impaired on that.

Zane just stood there, leaning on the wall by the bathroom, silently observing as I tried to take off my strappy high heels while singing the chorus, and fell over on the bed.

"See?" I kicked the shoes off and did my best to make it look like I'd meant to sit down. "Every word."

"Uh-huh."

"So?" I stared at him expectantly. "Don't you think if I was wasted, that would be the very, very first thing to go?"

His lips quirked. "That doesn't make much sense, Maggie."

"Yes it does!" I jumped to my feet. "Come on! Sing along. It won't sound as terrible if you sing it."

"Can't do it." He shook his head slowly. "Promised you I'd never sing that song."

Shit. That was true.

"Fine. But we're not just calling it a night! I'm all amped up, and it's your fault."

"My fault?"

"Uh, yeah. You're the one who dragged me out of bed and took me out on the town, married me, poured booze down my throat, bought me lap dance lessons, and sang karaoke to me. Now I'm not sleepy. Party with me."

"Jesus," he muttered. "Never thought I'd see the day."

"What day?"

"The day you begged me to party with you."

"Whatever." I paced to the other side of the room, but something snagged at me, drawing me back. "Wait. Wait just a sec…" I walked over to him, poking him in the chest. "Did you encourage me to drink all that booze so you wouldn't touch me?" I looked down at myself and wondered how drunk I looked. "Is this like… Zane repellent, or something?"

He laughed shortly, but the look in his blue eyes was much less than funny.

Yeah. I'd hit that one on the head.

Motherfucker had gotten me drunk on purpose so he wouldn't fuck me.

"Shit. You're such a dick!"

"How am I a dick? You wanted to have some champagne, and why shouldn't you? Why should you have to deal with Dizzy sober?"

"Exactly!" I was so thrilled that he saw it the same way I did, I tossed myself against him, slapping my hands on his chest. "Come on, Zane! Get over it. I promise I won't grope you. I just can't go to bed right now. I'll just lay there eating all those chocolates and being pissed at Dizzy and that's fucking stupid."

He studied me, a bunch of shit going on behind his eyes that I couldn't fathom. "Not worried about you groping me, Maggs."

"Okay. Well, I'm not gonna let you grope me either. I'm not

that drunk." I wasn't totally sure that I wasn't, but whatever. "Just… I don't know… get your shit together and smoke a joint or something, man. I need you."

His gaze slithered down my chest. I was still leaning on him, my breasts crushed against him. "Sure you want me to do that, babe?"

"Why not?" I asked casually, stepping back to put some space between us.

"Because I get horny as fuck when I smoke up."

He wasn't kidding. I could hear it in his voice. Could see it on his face.

But I wasn't some innocent victim here. I could keep my panties on if I wanted to.

I'd already kept them on for six years.

"You already smoked up when we were on the patio tonight, remember? And you managed to keep control of yourself."

"Right," he said. He was already pulling out his weed to roll a joint, as he studied me with one eye closed. "But I did ask you to marry me."

Chapter Nine

Maggie

S ometime later, Zane had smoked up, and I'd helped him. My eyeballs felt fuzzy and everything seemed really good.

Life was good, right?

I had the best job *in the world*. Every day I got up and I felt grateful for where I was. I had the respect of my coworkers, and I kicked ass at what I did. I knew I was appreciated. Needed.

So what if my dad didn't see what I was worth?

Maybe my "marriage" to Zane would change that. Fundamentally, it probably wouldn't. I'd just have to work harder at accepting it.

I wasn't going to change Dizzy Bowman. The man was an old, old dog, with no interest in picking up any new tricks.

And so what if I had no real girlfriends outside of work? I could always make new friends.

Besides… I had Zane. And right about now, that was all I really needed.

What else could I possibly need?

When he and I were together—and not pissing each other off

—it just fit. It felt right. At least, when he wasn't trying to get up my skirt.

Thing was, these moments were few and far between.

Maybe that was the only real problem between us.

We sat side by side, close together on the big white bed. We'd managed to have an extremely engaging conversation about Hanna-Barbera cartoons, the kind of conversation where time just cruises on by and I, for one, didn't even notice. I was vaguely aware that the sun would be coming up soon. We'd just had a heated, nonsensical argument about who would drive the car if we lived in the time of *The Flintstones*—uh, obviously we both would; it took a lot of feet to move those stone wheels, right?— and which dinosaur would make the best pet.

How we got onto *The Flintstones*? I asked Zane if he'd ever thought about marrying a woman before he popped the question out on the patio. I really thought the answer would be no. But after what appeared to be careful consideration, he said, "Betty Rubble."

A while later, once we'd agreed to disagree about the dinosaurs, I said out of nowhere, "She already had a husband."

Zane looked confused. "Huh?"

"Betty."

"Betty who?"

I laughed, and I couldn't stop laughing. It felt so fucking good to talk about nothing at all. Forget my dad. Forget this whole fucked-up night. Forget this unbearable sexual tension that had me all tied in knots every time I was alone with Zane.

I could live with it. All of it.

As long as Zane had my back, I could put up with anything, really.

Which reminded me of something. "What did my dad say to you?" I sat up straight and turned to face him. "When we were getting out of the limo and Maxxi hugged me, he leaned in and you guys were talking for a minute. What were you saying?"

He held my gaze, his eyes a little hooded, and I couldn't tell what he was thinking. Couldn't tell if he was stoned or not. "He was asking me for a meeting."

"Seriously? Jesus Christ," I practically growled. "Fuck! I can't believe he asked you that on our wedding night."

Zane said nothing, but a gorgeous smile crept across his face.

"What?" I elbowed him sharply.

"Nothing," he said.

"What did you tell him?"

"I said we'd meet. Day after tomorrow."

"What, here? In Vegas?"

"Yup."

I blinked at him. "You're on a flight at like eight in the morning. No way Dizzy's up early enough for that."

"Yeah," he said, unconcerned.

Slowly it started to penetrate my foggy brain. "You're really meeting up with him like you said you would?"

He shrugged. "This is my wedding night. I'm all high on nuptial ecstasy. Already forgot what he and I talked about." He cocked his head like he was trying to pull up some distant memory. "Did I even talk to Dizzy?"

I smiled, big time. "You are one damn good husband, Zane Traynor."

"Always knew I would be." His eyes were locked on mine, and he was so close I could feel his breath on my face. When did we get so close? I became aware of my hand, which I'd planted on his thigh at some point, but I didn't remove it.

His gaze dropped to my lips and lingered there.

I glanced down and away, because I couldn't keep looking at his face.

"You have beautiful feet," I whispered.

I could see them now, sticking out the legs of his frayed jeans, naked, his strong, graceful toes wiggling with latent energy. Like a tiger's tail twitching just before it pounces. When I looked back up he was cocking an eyebrow at me. Shit. I just said that out loud?

Right... now I remembered the other reason I made it a practice never to drink too much in Zane's company.

He licked his lips. "You say one more thing like that, Maggie May, and I'm gonna kiss you. Consider yourself warned."

"What? About your feet?"

"About my anything."

Turned out I didn't have to say a thing. I just kissed him first.

I really couldn't say what I was thinking when I climbed onto the bed with him; when I snuggled up to him like he was some asexual man-friend with innocent cuddling privileges, instead of a diabolical, sex-hungry man-whore with a permanent hard-on.

I couldn't say what I was thinking when I kissed him, either. If I was thinking at all.

Apparently I'd had just enough booze and pot and weirdness over the course of the night to allow myself to go there. For once, not to question his motives or worry about what this meant or warn myself I was making the world's most massive mistake.

I just leaned in and laid one on him.

His lips were soft and gentle in a way I didn't expect. It kinda took my breath away.

When we'd kissed just before the wedding ceremony, and during, those were hungry, passionate kisses. The first a slow burn, the latter a blazing fire. Maybe they were for show. I couldn't honestly tell which was the real deal; this kiss or those. Or maybe all of the above. But I fell into it, this kiss. I tilted my head a little when he pushed in deeper, opening for him. He swirled his tongue against mine, tentatively, and when I responded with a little moan I didn't even know was coming, he took my face in his hands and cranked up the heat.

After that, I had no idea what happened.

I lost track of myself in the ensuing inferno.

We were horizontal on the bed, making out like animals, and Zane's shirt was gone. Maybe it had incinerated. Somehow I was underneath him, and his hands were working their way up under my dress... and I didn't want to be anywhere else.

"Fuck... Maggie... I've wanted you... wanted this... for so long..."

He devoured me with his kisses, feasting on my mouth, my face, groaning when I kissed him back... and as I gasped for air in between—because I'd pretty much forgotten how to breathe—an awful, horrible thought invaded my brain.

What if any of this passion was about the booze?

I broke away, panting, lightheaded and breathless.

Sure, I'd brushed my teeth. Like that could magically undrink the booze I'd drank? The truth was, I was a lot less sober than I'd let on. I was pretty sure Zane knew that.

But that meant he was breaking *his* rule for me. And his rule was a big one. As in, his life pretty much depended on it.

Booze and women together... that's a temptation I just can't hack.

Shit.

Just... *shit.*

All the air squeezed from my lungs and my heart kicked in a really weird way.

I could *not* be the reason Zane destroyed his life.

Wait.

My *heart?*

When the hell did my heart get in on this?

Fuck me. My heart was *not* allowed to do weird kicky things for Zane.

It was *Zane*.

He was looking at me, his blue eyes hazy, his face a little flushed, his skin kinda dewy as his tongue swiped the corner of his mouth. I tasted his salt as I bit my lip.

When did it get so bloody hot in here?

"What's wrong?"

"I think you were right," I whispered, my hand on his chest as I pushed him away.

He didn't let go.

"I'm right about a lot of things, babe. Be more specific."

He slid his hand around my neck and dug his fingers into my hair, pulling me closer, and I said, "Maybe we shouldn't do this."

He stopped dead and stared at me. "You serious?"

I nodded. I was dead serious.

"Fuck me."

He released me and rolled away, sitting on the edge of the bed, facing away from me. Then he got up, fast, and put his shirt back on.

Shit. Was he pissed?

Where did he get off being pissed?

I scrambled off my side of the bed. "You weren't going to before, so why should I?"

He turned and stood glaring at me. I was actually glad the bed was between us, because he was starting to look stabby again.

"Because you *want* to."

"*You* want to," I shot back.

He clawed his hand through his blond hair, clearing it from his face. "For fuck's sake, woman, I've wanted to for six fucking years, and now you marry me and you still say no?"

"*You* said no."

"I'm saying *yes*," he said, with a not-so-subtle adjustment of his dick in his jeans.

"Because you *married* me."

"What the fuck does that mean?"

"It means this was all your idea!"

He shook his head. Then he rounded the bed so he could glare at me up close and I backed up until I hit wall.

"And you said yes to it," he said slowly, and really fucking quietly. "Right after I told you you weren't gonna pull this shit, remember?"

"I said yes because I hate my dad, Zane."

"You do not hate your dad."

"Yeah, I do."

He took a breath, turned away like he was looking for something to pummel, then turned back and stared me down again. "We just got married, Maggs—"

I rolled my eyes. I couldn't help it.

"We just got *married*," he repeated, leaning down close to my face. "Which means you're not gonna do that. You're not gonna lie to me. You're not gonna roll your eyes at me anymore. No more fucking wall of Maggie between us. Just *you* and *me*." He stepped in closer, until we were almost nose-to-nose. "You gonna look me in the eye right now and tell me you hate Dizzy?"

Shit. It really could be maddening as all hell the way the man saw through me.

And right now? Totally fucking inconvenient.

"No," I said softly, swallowing.

"Now do you wanna fuck or not?"

"Well... yeah."

"Good." He grabbed my face in both hands and pressed in close. "Because I'm gonna fuck you in about one minute, on those white satin sheets, and then I'm gonna do it again, and you're gonna fucking love it and I don't want you pissed off at me tomorrow."

Then he kissed me, and he was right.

I did love it.

Zane

The one thing I knew I would never forget, the moment that branded itself into my bones, was that first kiss after we were married.

As soon as the guy said the word, I'd claimed Maggie's sweet mouth with my own and thrust my tongue inside, making her mine. Officially. *Mine.*

My wife.

My Maggie.

And that stuff about never letting her go? I'd meant it.

No idea if she knew how much I meant it.

Didn't matter.

With Maggie, I'd always played the long game.

Just didn't realize until tonight that it was time for me to cash out.

Everything I'd ever wanted to do to Maggie, I was finally gonna do it. Now.

Kiss her all over. Devour her.

Totally unleash on her.

I was gonna fuck her until she rasped my name, her husky voice raw from screaming.

But first, I was just gonna kiss her. So I got her on the bed and that's what I did.

Lot of other things I wanted to do with my mouth, lot of places to explore, but I couldn't tear myself away from her lips.

Didn't even care that she'd been drinking. I should've cared. I just didn't. Didn't care about a thing but screwing her, hard. With my tongue. With my entire body. I rammed myself against her, fully dressed, just savoring the fact. Just drenching my senses in her.

I was gonna make Maggie mine in every fucking way I could think of before the sun came up.

"Zane... are you sure...?" she murmured against my lips, and I shook my head at her.

"Just shut up Maggie. For once in your life, just shut the fuck up and trust me."

Then I tore off her little pink dress and looked at her. I felt kinda breathless as I swiped my hair out of my eyes and stared at her.

She lay there breathing hard and staring back up at me. Just waiting for me.

Zane repellent? I almost laughed out loud. No way this woman could repel me.

Yes, I'd tried to get her drunk. Only because I thought it would keep me from taking advantage of her when she was feeling so low.

When we'd set out to the chapel, fucking right, I was planning on getting her into bed before the night was through. But then I saw how it was with her and Dizzy. She just wanted him to give a fuck, and the guy was blind to it. That, or he didn't know how to give a fuck. It hurt her. And I couldn't be a part of anything that hurt Maggie.

But now? There was nothing in her eyes but longing. Anticipation.

Desire.

I peeled her lacy bra and panties off. I just wanted to see her. All of her. She was so fucking pretty. And so strong. Her skin so smooth and soft... I started kissing her, nibbling her, licking every part of her body. I just needed to taste her, to inhale her sweet smell and get lost in her.

She could've done anything, said anything, fought me tooth and nail, and I would've wanted her.

She could've drank all the booze in Las Vegas.

Wouldn't matter.

This girl was my fucking kryptonite.

Right now, feeling her panting, getting hot beneath me, I would've done anything, given anything, risked anything to be with her.

Her breaths came faster, shorter, harder as I sucked her nipple into my mouth. As I teased her with my teeth. I had no idea if she was already regretting this. I hoped not, but I wasn't gonna let her dwell on it either.

I reached down and smoothed my fingers over her pussy. She was soft and wet. Hot. I let her nipple go and clenched my teeth as the hunger rocked through me. I was so fucking hard for her. Again.

Always.

I pressed my fingertip into her and she tensed.

"No. Wait," she gasped, reaching to stop my hand. Her gray eyes found mine, bright and clear. "I want your cock to be the first thing inside me."

She didn't have to tell me twice.

I got up and stripped off my clothes. Dug around in my pockets for a condom.

I sheathed my dick and went to her, and I gave her what she wanted. I didn't get her ready or tease her at all. I just filled her in one fast, possessive thrust that made her cry out.

Her fingernails dug into my ass as I fucked her and everything started to rush.

I was gonna come.

Way too fucking fast.

But Maggie was clawing at me, moaning and gasping, pulling me deeper, and no way I could stop. Pretty sure I couldn't hold on like this... maybe not the first time... maybe this one would be too fucking quick, and I'd just have to apologize and make it up to her later.

Fuck me. What a lousy fucking lay.

Then she surprised me by pushing me off. I rolled, taking her with me. Maggie straddled me, dug her knees into the bed, and started riding me, hard.

Hottest thing I'd ever seen.

"Oh, fuck," she said, wiggling around. "These stupid satin sheets!" Her knees were slipping all over the place.

"You wanna do it on the floor, babe?" I managed to rasp out. The repositioning had interrupted the rush, so I was able to hang on. But watching Maggie's tits bounce, feeling her hot pussy bear down on my dick? No fucking way.

I was not gonna last.

"My room," she gasped. Then she was up, and dashing across the hotel suite. I lay there for a second, kind of stunned.

Then I went after her, grabbing her around the waist and throwing her over my shoulder. She squealed in surprise and I slapped her ass. Hard. I took her into her room and tossed her on the bed. We came together and fell on our sides, kissing and fucking and kind of struggling for dominance.

She wanted on top.

I wouldn't let her mount up.

Not until I'd pounded her for a while and she got a little glassy-eyed and gave in. When she softened, I rolled over and drew her on top again. I couldn't take much more of that anyway.

She put her hands on my shoulders and rode me, slowly. Teasing me.

"You're gonna come when I say," she said softly, her eyes locked on mine. Her hair was all wild and in her face and spilling over her shoulders. Her lips were swollen.

I'd never seen anything more beautiful.

"Am I?"

"Yeah," she breathed, then bit her lip. "It'll make me come."

She rode me faster, jerking her hips as she found the friction she wanted. Then she got rougher, fucking me a lot harder than I expected her to.

"Jesus... Maggie..." I said between my teeth.

"Let's just get it out of the way," she said. "I can't wait anymore."

"Uh... yeah..." I rasped out. "But you should go first."

"Nuh-uh," she said. "Trust me. Next time, we can take our time..."

I wasn't gonna argue with that. Whatever the fuck she wanted... I just wanted to be there when it happened.

Anyway, it wasn't gonna take long for her to get her wish.

The pressure was building in my balls, hot and fast. My cock hummed as she squeezed me, aching for release as she slithered up and rammed down. She pulled almost completely away and swirled her hips, teasing my cockhead. I groaned desperately, clutching at her hips, and when her eyes caught mine, she said, "Now, Zane." Then she dropped down on me, hard. "Come for me."

I did. I blew so fucking hard I lifted her off the bed. I crushed her hips down to mine, squeezing her tight. My fingers dug in... pretty sure I left bruises.

She didn't complain.

She tossed her head back and moaned, and I felt her spasm, clenching around me as she rammed down a few more times, taking what she needed.

Then I grabbed her and spun us around, pressing her down beneath me, driving her into the pillows as I buried myself in her and rode out the aftershocks. When I did that, she came again, shuddering in my arms, gasping and clawing at me and crying my name.

Afterward, she blinked up at me with that gorgeous haze in her gray eyes as she went all soft and limp.

I kissed her deep as I held her. When I came up for air, I breathed with her.

Then I kissed her again.

I just wanted to stay lost in her. To feel nothing but her, taste nothing but her... stay inside her as long as I could.

Then I wanted to start all over at the beginning... and do it all again.

And again.

And again.

Chapter Ten

Maggie

R elieved.

That's how I felt when I woke and found Zane in bed with me. Naked.

For that uncomfortable moment teetering in the unreality between sleeping and wakefulness, the events of the night replayed in my head in a high-speed rush—all of them. And for a split second as I opened my eyes, I was intensely sure that none of it was real.

I'd dreamed it. All of it.

When I saw him lying next to me on his back, his head turned away, his chest rising and falling as the rhythm of his deep breaths sounded softly in the near-dark... yeah. I was glad he was here.

I was glad the whole crazy thing was real.

As I watched him, I couldn't help but feel a little happy.

Maybe sanity was overrated?

Maybe it was okay to go a little crazy, just for one night.

Then he turned his head and looked at me. He blinked his blue eyes, then locked on me.

Oh, shit.

I now knew that look. Intimately.

He rolled toward me. His warm hand found my stomach beneath the sheet and slid down, down... When his fingertips grazed my clit, I bit my lip to keep from gasping. I spread my legs without thinking.

Because hell, yes... I wanted more.

More of what I'd had last night.

In my defense, I was still only half-conscious, and besides, only a stupid, stupid woman would kick Zane Traynor out of bed. Only a crazy woman would let him into her bed in the first place, but still.

His eyes seemed to darken in the dim light and his hand slid further down, his fingers slicking against my already-wet flesh. Then he slipped inside, filling me. His fingers curved and undulated, doing insanely pleasurable things to my insides, and I moaned.

Okay. I was definitely awake now.

He repositioned himself above me and kissed me. His lips were hot and by this point, familiar. I liked how they felt against mine. How he sucked on my bottom lip and made soft growling noises low in his throat when he did it, like he couldn't help it. How he breathed faster and faster the more we kissed, like he was speeding toward the edge, and I was taking him there.

He slipped a second finger in to join the first, twisting both fingers around as he fucked me with them. I squirmed and moaned, unable to resist the almost-overwhelming pleasure. It just felt so good.

So. Fucking. *Good.*

I should've put a stop to it right here.

A smarter Maggie, a Maggie of twenty-four hours ago, would have. But she wouldn't have been in bed with Zane in the first place.

Which meant she would've missed out on this unbelievably pleasurable bliss.

But, yes. I should've stopped it. Last night was one thing.

A separate, one-time thing.

A crazy ending to a fucked-up night, prompted by hours of built-up, pent-up sexual tension. I'd been ditched mid-foreplay by Coop, and I was pissed off at my dad. I'd been humiliated and hurt. I was a little high. And a lot drunk.

But now? What excuse did I have for letting him do this to me?

I was no longer drunk. Not even a bit.

In the dim morning light, I was as stone-cold sober as it could get, and still I spread my legs for Zane.

I writhed and undulated beneath him, screwing his hand, wanting more. Even as I did it, I knew I was overthinking things. Zane had warned me not to do that. Actually, he'd kind of ordered me not to.

Well, fuck that. I didn't follow his orders.

I pushed him up and off, throwing one leg over him and shoving him down on his back, straddling him. His fingers were still inside me, and I rode them with all the pent-up frustration I still had left. There was a lot of it, apparently. Maybe until last night, when I'd fucked Zane—three times—I'd never realized how hard I held things in. Didn't realize it until I actually let loose and it all came rushing out.

So. Much. *Tension.*

He wrapped his hand around the back of my neck and pulled me down to him, kissing me fiercely as I kept riding his hand. The man had a wicked, talented tongue... but I gave back everything I got. I ravaged him, sucked on him, ate him alive, taking everything that was mine in this moment with my lips, my tongue and my teeth. It was hot and wet and all kinds of greedy. It was messy.

It was chaos.

It was becoming addictive.

It was only a few hours since we'd fallen asleep, but technically it was kind of a new day. The day I was supposed to get off my masochistic ass and get my shit together. Deal with the last night of the tour. Wrap things up with Brody and fly home. Say goodbye to the band, for now.

Say goodbye to Zane.

I'd see him again in a few months, when promotion for Jesse's solo album, which was coming out soon, really ramped up.

Maybe even before that.

But between now and then? Zane would do what Zane did. He could be with a hell of a lot of other women. I had no claim on him, despite what happened last night.

I didn't want a claim on him. Or so I kept telling myself, again and again, last night in the dark, as we claimed each other... again and again.

But we were here right now, and he was willing. There was nothing standing between us anymore. No one else, no booze, no distractions... other than my busy brain. Here, in the near-dark... it was just me and Zane.

And no one ever had to know.

What happens in Vegas...

I was moaning, kind of panting into his mouth as I neared orgasm. He felt it. I knew he felt it as I bore down on his fingers. He groaned and rolled me over, pinning me again as his fingers dug in and his thumb pressed my clit. It almost hurt, and I wanted it to. I just kissed him harder, pulling him down to me.

He withdrew his fingers and climbed on top of me and I braced for the thrust of his cock. Just once more. Once more and then we'd go back to our lives. He'd go back to screwing everything with a pussy—except me—and I'd go back to screwing the odd random hot guy who crossed my path, up to and perhaps including the occasional rock star... so long as it wasn't the one currently on top of me, seizing my wrists and pulling my hands up above my head, claiming me, again, with his mouth, his possessive kisses.

Shit, but that was a depressing thought. Way more depressing than it should've been.

He nudged my knees apart and settled between my legs, and as I opened for him, he rammed into me with an urgency that startled me, just like that first time. I gasped in pleasure-pain as my body stretched to take him. All of him. Zane did not hold back in this, or in anything he did. This was pure Zane, and it was beautiful and it was messy and it was perfect.

His blue eyes found mine and I just nodded, breathless, for him to keep going.

He fucked me hard and slow, pinning me there against the bed, churning into me with his hips the way I'd fantasized about him doing a hundred thousand times as I wrapped my legs around him and took him.

I felt tears prick at the corners of my eyes.

It was all so overwhelming.

Suddenly he stopped and withdrew, letting my wrists go as he crawled down my body. Then his tongue found my pussy and it was all over—any over-thinking, any kind of thought at all... rational or otherwise.

He lapped the flat of his tongue over my sensitive flesh once, twice, three times, and I relaxed into the bed. Then he focused on my clit, flicking the tip of his tongue lightly over it, then swirling around, and I shuddered, gasping for breath. After the rough treatment of his hand, the warm, gentle caresses of his tongue, soft and slick, were almost too much.

"Ah... Zane..." I gasped out, my voice all raw from last night, "... I can't..."

I didn't know why I said it. I just did.

"Maggie." He fluttered his tongue against me and practically growled. "Gonna make you come so hard…" And then he did. With one long, slow lick that set me off like a rocket. I arched and cried out, my voice raw and rasping. "Fuck, I love your voice," he murmured against my flesh as I came down.

Then he was at it again, teasing me to climax, taking his time, taunting and exploring, experimenting as he assaulted my clit with what felt like a thousand different types of licks, nibbles, kisses and strokes from every direction. I went off again and again, until he finally rose above me on his knees, panting.

He braced his hands on either side of me and lowered his hips, stroking the long, hard shaft of his cock against my pussy… and I exploded again, coming so hard as he ground against my clit that I bit my tongue.

"Oh my God," I panted. "Shit. I bit my tongue."

"You bleeding?" His brow creased with concern as he slowed his teasing thrusts and I shuddered, still coming down off that last orgasm.

"No." I poked my tongue around my mouth. "Just… ow."

He smiled and leaned down to kiss me softly. Then he lifted my limp legs by my thighs, spreading me wide, and thrust into me. I was so sopping wet by now that even as big as he was, his cock filled me in one smooth motion. No friction this time, no pain. Just slippery wet and heat. He shoved himself in to the root, then started rocking his hips, pumping himself slowly in and out. I met his thrusts, lifting my hips off the bed as he picked up speed, making him lose his rhythm in ragged breaths.

Then I was on top of him again, riding him with abandon, and then we were tumbling onto the floor. Zane managed to shove a blanket from the bed underneath me, more or less, and then he was pounding into me, hard. Unlike the bed, the floor had no give, and his pounding thrusts felt like punishment. It was a punishment I could take. I wanted it. I wanted him. I wanted him to tear me apart.

His whole body tensed as his breathing got rougher. His dazed blue eyes met mine as he started to come. *"Zane..."* I rasped his name as his cock jerked inside me.

He growled, low and strained in his throat. "Maggie," he gasped as he erupted. *"Fuck... Maggie..."* He pounded into me a few more times, sloppily, completely losing himself.

I came then, suddenly, his messy, desperate thrusts sending me over the edge again... writhing under him as he buried his face in my neck.

"Jesus... shit," he panted when it was over.

It wasn't eloquent, but yeah, that kinda summed it up.

We were both soaking wet. My whole body throbbed with my heartbeat, every nerve humming and alive.

We lay there a long time, entangled, until the sweat on my body cooled and I started to get cold. He felt me shiver and got up, tugging me to my feet.

As I flopped back onto the bed, I made the mistake of glancing in the direction of the bedside table. My phone was lighting up.

I took Brody's call as Zane went to the bathroom to clean up. It was only then that it struck me he'd been wearing a condom. Well, shit. Thank God one of us had been thinking.

But leaving that kind of thing up to Zane? Not a smart move.

Not smart at all.

Luckily the chat with my boss kept me from examining that too closely. Especially when he wanted to know why his Twitter feed was blowing up with a bunch of cell phone videos of Zane serenading me and my dad with "Rebel Yell" at a karaoke joint last night, and also, why he wasn't invited to that little party. I sputtered through my response to that, at which he sounded amused, and mercifully turned the conversation to other business.

After I got off the call, I thumbed through my new texts, including a link from Brody to one of the aforementioned videos, which I clicked on and watched for about three seconds before Zane came back out of the bathroom. He cocked an eyebrow at me as I stuffed the phone under my pillow.

Pretty sure he caught a snatch of the song though, and his own voice, not to mention all the lustful screaming in the background; there was a lot of it, more than I'd been aware of at the time, since when Zane Traynor took a stage, all else pretty much ceased to exist for me... and judging by that screaming, similar to the screaming that could be heard anytime he took a stage, I was not the only woman with this reaction.

I was wondering if I should just get it over with and do the naked morning-after dash to the bathroom, to avoid the awkward aftermath, when I realized I didn't need to. Instead of heading for the door with some lame excuse for needing to disappear, Zane sauntered over and sprawled on the bed next to me, face-down.

Like it was totally normal for him to sprawl out on a bed next to me, buck naked.

King of cool.

I should've gotten up and gotten dressed. Brody wanted to meet for breakfast in half an hour, and it would've been suspicious if I'd begged out. So I didn't.

It also gave me the perfect excuse to get out of here.

But Zane didn't seem to be in a hurry.

I really meant to get up. But somehow, I didn't budge.

Instead I listened to Zane's even, relaxed breathing as his beautiful feet played lazy footsie with mine.

And then, because I needed to say something to fill the air and distract myself from this growing awkwardness that was an uncomfortable mashup of embarrassment, confusion and guilt, I said, "I can't believe Elle missed our big fat fake wedding. She would shit."

"Thought you didn't wanna tell anyone," he mumbled into his pillow, the long blond strands of his hair scattered across his face.

"I don't." I reached up and smoothed the hair back with my fingertips, gently, so I could see him. I wouldn't be able to touch him like this in an hour or two, so why not? Might be my last chance.

The one eye I could see was closed, his eyelashes long and straight, nearly black at the root, lightening to golden-blond at the tips. Yeah, Zane had beautiful eyelashes. Was there anything about the man that wasn't beautiful?

Nope. I would know. Got up close and incredibly personal with every last inch of him last night, and I sure as hell couldn't find it.

He stirred a little as I let my fingers trail down his temple and around his ear where the hair, buzzed short, felt like velvet. That one blue eye opened as I brought my hand away, and froze on me.

"Fake?"

"How long should we wait to tell my dad it wasn't real?" I wondered aloud. "I mean... we can't just let him believe it forever, much as I'd love to let him dangle..." It would be cruel and pretty shitty of me to lie to my dad for any length of time, and I knew it. But after what he'd said to me yesterday... my own father called me a slut, for fuck's sake. I was prepared to let him dangle for a little while.

Hell, for all I cared we could wait until after he sent us our wedding gift. It would be something expensive, knowing Dizzy. Not out of generosity, but because he'd consider it poor form to send Zane a wedding gift that was anything less than seriously, grandiosely overpriced.

Maybe I was a terrible person, but the thought of parting

Dizzy with any of his precious money made me smile. Damn right, he could send us a gift. And we weren't returning it, either.

Zane lifted up, still eying me strangely, and rolled onto his side. His legs were all tangled up with mine from the knee down. I focused on his face to avoid looking at his cock, which was now in full view.

He blinked at me, his eyes adjusting to the pale morning light, like he wasn't sure if he was seeing things right.

"It was real," he said slowly but really quietly, and the smile dropped from my face.

Zane Traynor had fucked with me plenty of times, and you better believe I knew when he was fucking with me.

He wasn't fucking with me now.

The intensity in his blue eyes said it all, as they burned into me with that look that could give you frostbite.

"No," I said, so calmly I kind of scared myself. I didn't even know where the words came from, but they were coming out of my mouth. "It. Was. *Fake.*"

"It wasn't fake."

"It wasn't *real*," I protested, my brain groping madly for an explanation that would make his words make sense.

"You thought it was fake?" he asked, his eyebrows drawing together in a dangerously pissed-off look.

What the fuck was happening?

"You thought it was *real?*"

"Why would it be fake?"

"*Why would it be real?*"

I jumped up, untangling Zane's naked body from mine and scrabbling off the bed, pulling the sheet with me as a shield.

"No. Nuh-uh. That was a pretend ceremony and you paid the chapel guy to… to…"

"To marry us?" he finished for me.

Oh. *God.*

"For fuck's sake, Zane! You *didn't*."

"Pretty fucking sure I did." He rubbed a hand over his face, looking sleepy and irritated as fuck.

Too fucking bad! He didn't get to be pissed at me. Not when he—

"Jesus!" I jabbed my left hand in the air. "These stupid cheap rings?"

He glanced from the ring to my face, looking unimpressed as shit, and cocked that wicked pierced eyebrow at me.

"These are supposed to be stupid cheap rings, Zane," I informed him, anger rising along with the panic. "Like pretend, 'Ha ha, I just fake-married my friend in Vegas because it's hilarious' rings."

"If you say so."

He started to drag himself up off the bed, giving me an eyeful of his godlike body and his stupid gorgeous dick.

"No. No, we did not. I did not. I couldn't have. I did not just *marry* you..." I babbled on, clinging to the sheet like a lifeline.

"Actually, sweetheart," he said, "you did. Maybe you remember that part where you said 'I do' or the paperwork we signed?"

He wandered out of the room, giving me an eyeful of his sculpted ass... then he returned, holding the vest he'd worn to our wedding last night. Our *fake* wedding. "I'm gonna take a shower," he said, sounding kinda disgusted as he dug something from the inside pocket of the vest and tossed it at me. "And by the way..."

It landed on the bed just in front of me.

A small, red velvet box.

A ring box.

"... there's your legit proposal."

Against my better sense, I picked up the box and opened it... to find a gorgeous platinum ring with a big-ass diamond staring me in the face.

Epilogue

Jesse

What a shitty fucking night.

I'd lain in bed, unable to sleep, for hours before I gave up on trying.

Zane invited me up to the penthouse to meet some girls, but I ignored his texts. Dylan wanted me to come down to the bar. I didn't go.

Instead I tried to watch a movie. I tried to write some music. I played guitar for a while, just trying to clear the argument with Elle from my head.

It had really pissed me off this time.

I wasn't fucking flirting with that chick. I was being friendly. Professional. I was pretty sure I'd know if I crossed a line, but lately, it seemed like everything I did went over some line with Elle.

I couldn't fucking take it anymore.

So I got up and went to the rooftop gym. I didn't want to be recognized. I just wanted to be alone. But I couldn't stand sitting in the hotel room any longer.

Luckily, the gym was pretty much empty.

I should've called Jude, probably. Talked it through. But I didn't call. I didn't text. I didn't want to talk; maybe I was through fucking talking. I was definitely through arguing with Elle over the same fucking things, over and again.

We just weren't working as a couple. Why couldn't she see that?

I went over and over it in my head as I worked out. But any way I looked at it, it was the same old thing. Elle and I were just too fucking different, in the ways that really counted, to make this thing work.

We could never work it out anyway, even when we tried. We couldn't even talk about shit without fighting. She got confrontational. I withdrew. She was quick-tempered. I was brooding.

To other men she was "passionate." To other women I was "mysterious."

We both drove each other crazy.

And she still loved me. I knew she did.

She always had.

That knowledge weighed like a rock in my gut. Because I knew she would do anything for me. For us.

When I was done at the gym, I paced through the hotel with my hood thrown up. It was the dead of night, and while it was Friday night in Vegas, the hotel corridors were pretty quiet.

I walked a long time, but there was nowhere for me to go to get away from this problem, and the problem was, Elle wanted more from me than I could give. She thought I was holding something back from her. Holding myself back.

Maybe I was.

I just didn't know.

But I wasn't looking to mess around with anyone else. I was just being me. That had never been enough for her, though. She just kept pushing and pulling, and it was bleeding me dry.

She wanted me to love her, unconditionally. I knew that. And it was a fair thing to want.

I just couldn't get there.

And I was tired of feeling shitty about it. Feeling guilty.

I just wanted to let it go.

I wandered toward the lobby. It was lined with a bunch of giant columns, interspersed with massive plants. I was coming through the columns lining the walkway that led into it, and that's when I saw them.

Zane, Maggie and Flynn, standing in the lobby.

They were with Maggie's dad, Dizzy. Dizzy had his arm around some girl and Zane had his arm around Maggie. Maggie looked drunk, and something made me stop short.

As they parted ways, I heard the chick with Dizzy say, "Farewell!" in a sing-song voice. She and Dizzy seemed to be heading for the bar. It was closed, but since he owned the place, probably not a problem. "Sleep tight, Mr. and Mrs. Traynor!" the girl shout-whispered across the lobby. Then Dizzy grabbed her hand and tugged her out of sight.

Mrs. Traynor?

I stared at Zane and Maggie, and it all came together in an instant. Las Vegas. The bouquet in Maggie's hand.

The fucking rings.

I could see them, glinting in the lights off the bank of elevators. Zane wore a lot of rings, so I couldn't be sure. But Maggie was definitely wearing a wedding band on her ring finger.

I saw it when she put her hand on his cheek.

What the *fuck*?

I watched them get in the elevator, leaning way too close together. Flynn stepped in silently behind them, and the doors closed.

They never saw me.

I wandered around a while longer. Then I went back to my

Dirty Like Us

room, poured myself a couple of fingers of bourbon and tried to absorb what I'd seen.

Totally impossible, and defying every law of the universe I'd ever heard of, but I was pretty fucking sure that Zane and Maggie had just gotten married.

Damn.

How long had this been going on? Were they fucking?

Of course they were fucking.

Were they in love?

Probably. That's usually what a wedding implied.

Weirdly, I could see it with Zane. Surprised he would ever marry anyone, and yet, I could see him falling for Maggie. He'd always had a thing for her. I just didn't know how serious it was, apparently.

Zane never seemed to take anything that serious. Wasn't really his style. But somehow... yeah, I could see him taking Maggie seriously.

Maggie, though? What the fuck was she doing marrying Zane?

Shit. I sat back on the bed and had to wonder... Should I be concerned? Should I say something to Zane? To Brody? Maggie had looked pretty drunk, weaving into the elevator in her high heels. Zane had been helping her along. I'd rarely seen her that drunk.

Fucking hell. I rubbed my hand through my hair and told myself it wasn't my problem. Not my business at all. So long as Zane didn't screw up what we had with Maggie. She was part of the team. Part of our family. He'd be in big fucking trouble if he fucked Maggie over.

There were a lot of people, me included, who'd have a problem with that.

I just hoped, for the band's sake, that he knew that.

Motherfucker.

127

I shook my head. But there was nothing to be done, not until they mentioned it. Maybe Zane would make an announcement at the show, on stage. Declare his love for Maggie in front of the world.

I grinned at the thought. It was actually kind of sweet.

Kinda shocking, but I was happy for them. So long as they were happy.

Anyway, I had problems of my own.

I went out on the balcony a while, looking out over the glittering city, and pondered it. Because Elle was family too, and I really didn't want to be the motherfucker who pissed everyone off.

Zane marries Maggie and I break up with Elle?

Who's the asshole now?

Shit. How would everyone react?

Would they be pissed at me?

We'd been in this band, together, for a decade. Elle, Zane, Dylan and I. And no one was gonna be happy about what I was about to do.

Least of all Elle.

But I had to do it.

I'd wait until after tomorrow's show, though. Tonight's show. It was after five in the morning; the tour would be over tonight.

The morning after the show, Elle and I were going to her place in L.A.. I was hoping to meet up with my sister when she got into town. Just planning to lay low. Write some music. Spend time with friends. Take a little break before the new album launch.

Now all I wanted to do was go home.

Have some time alone.

I was so *fucking* tired.

I collapsed into bed near dawn, feeling like I could finally sleep because the decision had been made, as difficult as it was.

As painful as this thing was gonna be.

It just had to be done.

When we got back to L.A., I'd sit Elle down. I'd ask Brody to set up a flight. Get me back to Vancouver by the end of the day. But before I left, I'd have to look her in the eye. I'd have to tell her.

We couldn't drag this out anymore.

I just couldn't do it another day.

When I woke, it was late morning and Jude had left a text. I'd missed our morning run.

There was a text from Elle, too. She wanted to talk. She said she was sorry.

As I stared at the words, a text came in from Dylan. He was hungry. As usual. He wanted to meet up for lunch.

I put the phone down. I felt groggy and over-tired. I'd slept five hours; it had been a heavy, dark, dreamless sleep, but as I gradually blinked my way to life, everything became so fucking clear.

I threw the curtains open. It was a blazing, gorgeous day. I looked down over the Strip. It was gonna be a killer fucking show tonight. I could feel it.

This band, the music, were my heart and my soul. And I loved my bandmates. I loved Elle.

But the hard truth was, I wasn't in love with her. Not like she was in love with me.

And not like she deserved.

I knew it with certainty as I showered and got dressed.

Zane had texted by then. The band was heading to a restaurant. I'd meet up with them for lunch. I'd be damned sure no one suspected anything was off. I'd be civil with Elle. She wouldn't push it.

She always knew I needed time to come back to center after a fight anyway. That was the advantage of a relationship with someone who knew you so well; they understood all your little flaws and weirdnesses.

Didn't mean they had to like them.

I texted Jude to meet me in the lobby and threw up my hood as I headed out the door. Yeah, tonight's show would be epic. I would never let what was happening with Elle and I overflow onto the band. I knew she wouldn't, either.

We would stay together, play together, always.

Just not the way Elle wanted.

There just wasn't enough chemistry between the two of us, in that way, to maintain that kind of bond, to get us past our differences through the highs and the lows of life, much less the life of a band on the road.

I needed something more.

Something else.

I didn't know what it was yet.

I just knew that when I found it... I would know it was the real thing.

THE END

Thank you for reading!

Don't miss **Dirty Like Me** and **Dirty Like Brody**,
the next book(s) in the Dirty series
—depending which book you started with!

Books by Jaine Diamond

For the most up-to-date list of Jaine Diamond's published books and reading order please go to
https://jainediamond.com/books/

Dirty Series

Dirty Like Me

Dirty Like Us

Dirty Like Brody

A Dirty Wedding Night

Dirty Like Seth

Dirty Like Dylan

Dirty Like Jude

Dirty Like Zane

Players Series

Hot Mess

Filthy Beautiful

Sweet Temptation

Lovely Madness

Flames and Flowers

Vancity Villains Series

Handsome Devil

Rebel Heir

Wicked Angel

DEEP Duet

DEEP (DEEP #1)

DEEPER (DEEP #2)

Never miss a book—join Jaine's **Diamond Club Newsletter**
at jainediamond.com to get new release info,
insider updates, giveaways and free bonus content.

Acknowledgments

A massive, heartfelt thank you to all the reviewers and bloggers who have embraced *Dirty Like Me (Dirty #1)* and this new series right out of the gate. You ladies and your love of books really, seriously rock. The kind, welcoming, enthusiastic, supportive and sometimes hilarious messages I find in my inboxes throughout the day *make* my day. I could not do this without you.

A big thank you goes to Marjorie and Guinevere for beta reading—once again, quickly and on short notice. You ladies are nothing short of awesome.

My deep appreciation goes to the many reviewers, readers, and friends who are passionately, humorously, sweetly and/or weepily requesting more books from me (asap!) on a daily basis. I LOVE that you're loving my stories and that you kindly take the time to tell me so! (Believe me when I say they are coming, as fast as I can possibly write them; knowing you're out there looking forward to them is a total gift. I promise more books are on their way, featuring many of your favorite characters!)

Big love to my partner, Mr. Diamond, for always being there for every single thing, no matter how big or how small. Thank you for being the first reader of this book, and for helping me make it better; you always do. I'm so thrilled we're on this crazy-awesome journey together.

To my readers: thank you to those of you who have already read and loved *Dirty Like Me* and wanted more of Zane and Maggie. It's thrilling to me that Zane and Maggie made an impression on you in their brief appearances in the first Dirty novel. I'm so honored that you chose to read this love story; my intent as a romance author is to spread love. As an independent author, I could not do what I do without you. If you've enjoyed Zane and Maggie's story so far, please consider leaving a review and telling your friends about this book; your support means the world to me.

With love and gratitude,
Jaine

Playlist

Love music like Zane & Maggie do? Me too!

Some of the songs on the *Dirty Like Us* playlist are mentioned in the book; others are songs that captured the feel of a certain scene or that I listened to while writing the book.

Like the music in all the Dirty series books, this playlist features mostly rock—from classic rock to hard rock and everything in between—but it also includes other genres that I, and the characters in the book, enjoy as well.

Turn. It. Up!

You'll find the links to the full playlists
on Spotify and Apple Music here:
http://jainediamond.com/dirty-like-us/

Magic Carpet Ride — Steppenwolf
You're Crazy — Guns N' Roses
Let's Get It On — Marvin Gaye

Woman — Wolfmother
Howlin' For You — The Black Keys
40 Day Dream — Edward Sharpe and the Magnetic Zeros
Do You Want To — Franz Ferdinand
Strange Days (Thievery Corporation Remix) — The Doors
Can't Buy Me Love — The Beatles
Rebel Yell — Billy Idol
Whole Lotta Love — Led Zeppelin
Just One of Those Things (Brazilian Girls Remix) — Blossom
Dearie

About the Author

Jaine Diamond is a Top 50 Amazon bestselling author of contemporary romance. She writes badass, swoon-worthy heroes endowed with massive hearts, strong heroines armed with sweetness and sass, and explosive, page-turning chemistry.

She lives on the beautiful west coast of Canada with her real-life romantic hero and daughter, where she reads, writes and makes extensive playlists for her books while binge drinking tea.

www.jainediamond.com

Join the readers' group Jaine Diamond's VIPs on Facebook to chat with Jaine and other readers.

Preview of Dirty Like Me

Don't miss the first full-length novel in the Dirty series,
Dirty Like Me—Jesse and Katie's story!

Dirty Like Me is a full-steam, fake-to-real romance, featuring a charming, famous heartbreaker, a sweet "regular" girl, a salacious job offer, a ridiculous bet and way too many shared hotel beds.

CHAPTER ONE

Katie

I didn't mean to crash the meeting.

I fully intended to knock before entering, like a civilized person. Max had other plans. For one thing he was a dog, and for another he knew we were dropping in on my best friend, Devi. Devi was a total babe, and Max totally dug hot babes. One glimpse of the door to her office, which was ajar, and he streaked past the front desk, big wet tail wagging, startling a couple of Devi's coworkers.

"On it!" I blurted, diving after him, but he'd already hip-checked the door open. By the time I caught up, my wayward black lab was shaking off his rain-wet fur in a flurry of excitement, spraying Devi and the three other people standing in her office. I made a mad grab for his collar.

I missed.

Hovering awkwardly on the threshold, I clutched the tin of miniature pies I'd been unpacking in the lobby and mouthed a *Sorry!* at my BFF.

"Hey, Katie!" Devi smiled brightly, tussling Max's ears with a friendly pat. "Max! Aren't you wet." She shot me a look that said something like, *Nice to see you, but what the hell?*

"Um... hi," I said. Devi was a talent agent; her agency repped models and actors, so I was used to running into beautiful people in her office. Though I didn't usually crash her meetings with my dog, wet and disheveled in my paint-stained jeans. "Sorry about my dog. Come on, Max." I gave Max the *get-your-furry-butt-over-here* look, a look he knew well but completely ignored, since Devi and her pretty female guest were now loving him up.

"No problem. We were just finishing up." Devi gestured for me to stay put, though I really just wanted to grab my delinquent dog and get the hell out of there. I felt ridiculously conspicuous in my white tank top, which I'd regretted wearing about two seconds after it started raining. As Devi wrapped things up with her guests, I took stock. Yep. Purple bra totally showing through my now-transparent tank.

Great.

Devi was shaking hands with the built dude in the short-sleeve button-down, and I noticed some tattoos on his muscular arm, but that was about it. My attention had already snapped to the other guy as some unconscious, primal part of me registered his hotness before the rest of me could catch up.

Plus, he was staring at me.

Or at least, my see-through shirt.

Devi strode to the door to see her guests out and I stepped aside, holding my tin of pies, trying to disappear into the wall. He was coming at me. Tall and broad-shouldered, his thick, dark hair in unkempt waves that gave him a decidedly just-fucked look, like some lucky bitch had just clawed through it. Totally worked on him. He wore a fitted black T-shirt, which I swore I could see his well-defined abs through, and ripped, dark jeans molded to his long, hard thighs...

My brain must have short-circuited, because my gaze got stuck on the package in the front of those jeans. When I looked up, his molasses-dark eyes were locked on mine. He stopped a foot in front of me and stared.

Fair enough, since he'd just caught me checking him out like a horny perv.

I cleared my throat, which was suddenly tight. "Pie?" I fumbled with the tin, lifting it between us, blocking his view of my bra. "They're cherry."

He glanced in the tin, where two dozen hand-crafted miniature pies were neatly arranged, my signature cherry filling peeking out through the crisscrossed pastry tops. Then his gaze lifted to mine again. He had the longest, darkest eyelashes I'd ever seen on a man. High cheekbones. Luscious, kissable lips. Strong jaw shadowed with dark stubble, like he hadn't shaved in days. And those beautiful dark eyes, smoldering at me and making me blush, big time.

"Maybe another time," he said, the deep, sexy rumble of his voice stirring parts of my anatomy that hadn't been stirred in a crazy long time. I noticed something tick against his teeth as he gave me a faint yet heart-stopping smile. A piercing?

No. Candy.

Cinnamon. His breath smelled like cinnamon.

I glanced over at Devi. She and the others were standing in the doorway, staring at us.

Max, ever the opportunist, snuffled into the hand of the hottest guy in the world as I stood there, dazed. I noticed the big, silver rings on his fingers as he stroked Max's velvety ears, and the tattoo on his wrist, a pair of dark wings wrapped around his strong forearm.

"Come on, Max." I pulled Max back so he could get by. "Sorry. He, um, likes you." Normally Max preferred the ladies, but I could hardly fault his taste.

The hottest guy on the planet said nothing. He didn't really get a chance before the ever-charming Devi intervened and herded all three of them out the door.

I set my tin of mini pies on Devi's desk, feeling kind of windblown, like I'd just stepped in out of a storm rather than a light Vancouver mist. Really, a girl should be warned before a guy that hot gave her the most thorough eye-fucking of her life.

Did I really offer him pie?

Cherry pie?

Ugh. So fucking smooth.

I tidied Max into an obedient ball on the rug beneath the desk and willed him to stay put as Devi returned, shutting the door behind herself.

"I know," she gushed. "So fucking hot, right?"

Um, yeah. But I knew better than to answer that honestly. The last time I casually inquired about a hot guy I glimpsed at my best friend's office, she took it upon herself to hook the two of us up on a blind date. And when a hot male model gets set up with someone he assumes will be some equally hot female model, but turns out to be just some regular girl, things do not go well. For the regular girl.

Luckily, Devi didn't even wait for my response. "Jesus, Katie." She strode over, a takeout coffee cup in each hand. "What the hell?"

"I know. Max just bolted for your office—"

"Not that." She gave me a no-contact air hug, then glanced down at my chest. "You look like a sexy drowned rat. Heard of an umbrella?"

"My hands were full."

Devi scowled. "Do not tell me you rode your skateboard in the rain. I hate it when you do that."

I rolled my eyes a little. My glamorous best friend had never understood my love affair with my skateboard. Of course, she drove a luxury SUV her parents bought for her and lived in her own suite in their giant house, so she didn't exactly relate to my thriftiness. In the case of my preferred mode of transportation, she just saw it as risky behavior. Unfortunately, my big sister agreed with her. "Becca already gave me the lecture when I stopped to pick up the coffees."

Devi set my cherry-vanilla latte on the desk with a little *harrumph* and eyed the mini pies with suspicion. "You've been baking."

"Just some pies." I flopped into one of the chairs facing the desk, which still had hot guy pheromones all over it. I sucked back a deep breath, savoring the lingering scents of cinnamon, leather, and the faint, intoxicating musk of a warm, clean male.

"Katie."

"What?" I glanced up; Devi was studying me accusingly.

"*Just* pie?"

"And some scones."

She raised a slender eyebrow.

"And a few cookies," I added.

"What flavor?"

"Chocolate chip."

"Uh-huh."

"And pecan butter ripple."

"I knew it. What's wrong?"

"Nothing."

"Bullshit. You look..." Devi looked at me sideways. "Horny."

"I am not horny," I lied. Who wouldn't be after getting eye-fucked like that? My head was still dangerously deprived of blood.

Devi sat down behind her desk. She looked gorgeous, as always, her dark hair smoothed out, flawless cappuccino skin set off with velvety red lipstick, sleeveless black top tricked out with a chunky necklace and leopard-print leggings, all of which she'd probably worn specifically for the meeting she'd just had. Fashion was just one of the many ways Devi built rapport with people.

I, on the other hand, considered myself coordinated if I managed to pull on matching shoes.

"Spill." She gathered up the slew of model photos that littered the surface of her desk, stuffing them into a file folder. "I've got like ten minutes before my next meeting. What's up?"

"Nothing. We just miss you." It was true; my best friend had been pulling a lot of overtime, which was great for her career but not so great for me.

"I miss you guys too." She reached beneath the desk and pet Max. "But that's not the reason you busted in here."

"Again, sorry. Just wanted to talk to you. I figured this may be my only chance to do it face-to-face."

"Talk about...?"

I took a breath and sighed. "I think... I may be ready."

Devi lit up, then caught herself and cooled her reaction. "Oh?" She was trying really hard not to jump for joy. It was kind of cute.

"I know you've been telling me this for a long time. I just had to get there myself."

"For sure."

"For so long I just wasn't ready, you know? And then maybe I was, sort of, but I was scared. And then it just got easy to keep avoiding it. But now…"

"Now?" Devi fluttered her dark eyelashes hopefully.

I sipped my latte. "Are you sure you have time for this?"

"Hell, yes."

"Okay. I think I need to go on a date."

"Halle-fucking-lujah!"

"Alright. Ugh. I'm so bad at this." Just saying it out loud to Devi made me nervous. Especially when she got all sparkly about it.

"What? Dating?" Devi sipped her coffee, waving a manicured hand in the air. "You always say that, but you never date. How do you get good at anything unless you practice?" She waggled her eyebrows, making me grin.

When it came to dating, Devi was a total pro. I, on the other hand, was pretty much a born-again virgin, more or less by default.

"You're going to meet someone who blows your lid off, babe. You just have to put yourself out there." Devi's cell phone buzzed and she glanced at the screen. "Oh! I should take this." She picked up. "Hey, Maggie!"

I wandered over to the stack of magazines on the coffee table. These days, I was getting used to sharing Devi with her other life. Just one more hint from the universe that I needed to get a life of my own.

I sank onto the couch and flipped through a French Vogue. Max came to lay at my feet and I toed his soft fur with my sneaker. Devi was such a natural with people. She'd forgotten more hot men than I'd ever dreamed of meeting. The concept of *not* putting herself out there wouldn't even cross her mind. But for me, the whole idea of exposing myself to rejection and failure made my stomach churn.

Still, she was right. I wasn't about to meet guys sitting at home with my dog.

Not like I hadn't tried.

"Okay? Oh. Okay..."

I glanced up at the odd tone in Devi's voice. Bad news? Her eyes met mine, but I couldn't quite read the look in them.

"Mm-hmm. Right. Okay... no, no problem. I totally understand." I went back to my magazine while she finished up the conversation, which was brief and consisted of a lot of "Totally," and "No problem," and "Of course."

I looked up again when Devi hung up. She was staring at her phone, like it might somehow explain to her what just happened. "Well. That was interesting."

"A client?"

"No. Maggie Omura. You just met her. Kind of."

"Oh." Right. The pretty dark-haired waif with the hot guy and the even hotter guy. "Max liked her. Didn't you, Max?" At the sound of his name, Max woofed contentedly.

Devi leaned back in her chair, assessing me. "You also just met Jesse Mayes, which you're playing it awfully cool about."

"Who?" I slurped whipped cream from the top of my coffee.

Devi sighed. "Honestly, Katie. Are you kidding me? Jesse Mayes?"

"What? That guy who just left?" I pretended to be enraptured with a deodorant ad in my magazine. "One of your models?"

"I wish. Jesse Mayes is only one of the hottest rock stars in the world and as an incredibly cool young person you should really know what I'm talking about."

I assumed she added the "incredibly cool young person" comment since last week we got into an argument when she said my apartment looked like an old lady lived in it. And after I'd rigidly defended my music collection (on vinyl), my home phone (on a cord), and my TV (which didn't exist), I realized she had a point, and maybe she was just scared of losing her best friend to spinsterhood at the age of twenty-four, which was probably a realistic fear.

I gave her my best stink eye anyway. "So?" Then I went back to my magazine, because in truth I had no idea who Jesse Mayes was. Other than the hottest guy in the known universe.

"So," she said, "I thought you liked Dirty."

"Dirty what?"

"The band. Dirty."

"Oh. Who doesn't?" I looked up again. "You mean, he's in that band?" I knew music. Kind of prided myself on it. But people? People were Devi's domain.

"He's their lead guitarist. And he sings like a sexy beast."

That, I could believe.

"He just put out a solo album and they're shooting a music video in town. The woman they cast to star in it with him as his music video girlfriend bailed." Devi tipped her pretty nose in the air. "Not from our agency, of course."

"Of course," I said, but she'd lost me somewhere around *sexy beast*. I was now trying to recall every Dirty song I knew, and imagining how Jesse Mayes would look playing guitar, and singing under a spotlight all covered in sweat.

"Anyway." Devi sipped her coffee, eying me over the rim. "Long story short. I met Maggie at a party a while back. She works with Dirty as the assistant to their manager, you know, the dude with all the tattoos."

Uh-huh. Hottie number two.

"She's involved in a lot of their publicity and whatnot and naturally we've been in touch."

"Naturally."

"She called me up last night. They're looking to recast, but they're having some issues getting Mr. Rock Star to commit to what he wants. Maggie knew they'd be in the neighborhood today, so she took the opportunity to haul his ass in here and have him choose one of our girls."

"That'll be some lucky girl." I kept flipping through the magazine, but I didn't really see the pages. I was too busy trying to picture Jesse Mayes with his shirt off.

"Exactly. They just hired one of our models."

"Well that's good for you, right?"

"It's great for me. Katie, pay attention." Devi stood, came around her desk and took the Vogue from my hands. "They changed their minds. They just called to drop her."

"Oh. Well, that's shitty." Why was Devi all up in my face about it?

She dropped the Vogue on the coffee table with a resounding splat. "They dropped her because they want *you*."

Preview of Dirty Like Brody

Don't miss the next book in the Dirty series,
Dirty Like Brody—Brody and Jessa's story!

Dirty Like Brody is an angsty, childhood-friends-to-lovers romance, featuring a broody, overprotective hero, a heroine tortured by the mistakes of her past, and a long overdue second chance.

———

PROLOGUE

Jessa

I will never forget the first time he spoke to me.

I remember everything, right down to the music that was playing on the Discman I had tucked into the back of my jeans. (It was my brother's new Chris Cornell album, and the song was "Can't Change Me.") When the bullies started taunting me I turned it up, but I still heard what they said.

I was eight years old, and the last girl on the playground anyone would ever guess would grow up to become a fashion model. Every day I came to school in clothes that were worn and usually a couple sizes too big for me, hand-me-downs, either from my brother or from Zane. When I wore their baggy clothes, the other kids didn't spend so much time telling me how skinny I was.

But they said other things.

I was sitting alone in the playground after school when it happened, up on top of a climbing dome; my brother and his friends called it "Thunderdome" because they'd made a game of dangling like monkeys from the bars inside and kicking the crap out of each other. The bullies were standing at the bottom of Thunderdome, so I couldn't even run away. They were big bullies. Fifth grade bullies, and while my brother, who was in seventh, would've intervened, he wasn't there.

"How come you got shit stains all over your jeans?" the dumb-looking one asked me, leaning on Thunderdome and looking bored. "Doesn't your mom do laundry?"

"You got a shit leak in those saggy diapers, dork?" the even dumber-looking one asked, and they both snorted.

"Yeah, she's so full of shit her eyes are brown."

"What's wrong, baby dork? You gonna cry?"

No. I wasn't going to cry. My brother had a lot of friends and while they were never *that* mean to me, twelve-year-old boys could be relentless. I knew how to hold my own. I'd cry later, at home, when no one could see me.

Besides… the new boy was coming over, and I definitely wasn't crying in front of him.

He was in seventh grade, but the rumor was that he was thirteen or even fourteen and had flunked a grade or two. Obviously, he was super cool. He wore an actual leather jacket, black with silver zippers, like rock stars wore. He smoked outside the school, hung out alone at the edge of the school grounds, and spent more time in the principal's office than the principal. I never knew what he did to get in trouble, but whatever it was, he did it a lot.

The other kids in my class thought he was scary. I just thought he was sad.

Ever since Dad died, I knew sad when I saw it.

The bullies saw him coming and they started getting squirrelly. I thought they'd run but he was there too fast, closing the distance with his leisurely, long-legged stride.

"You guys're so interested in shit, there's some over here I can show you, yeah?" He stood with his hands in his pockets, his posture relaxed, as the bullies started going pale.

I slipped my headphones off.

"Naw, I don't wanna—"

"Sure you do, it's right over here." He toed the ground at his feet with his sneaker. The grass was still damp from a bit of rain in the afternoon and mud squished out.

The bullies started shaking and sniveling, babbling apologies and excuses. There was a brief, almost wordless negotiation, at the end of which they ended up on their knees in front of him.

He hadn't moved. His hands were still in his pockets.

"Just have a little taste and tell me if it's fresh," he told them, in a tone that brooked no argument, squishing his foot in the muck again.

Then he looked up, his brown hair flopping over one eye, and winked at me.

I stared from my perch atop Thunderdome with unabashed, eight-year-old awe as the bullies bent forward, shuddering.

He was going to make them eat shit!

For me!

I was ninety-nine-point-nine percent sure it was just wet mud, but those bullies were scared enough to believe it. And ate it, they did.

He then told them to apologize to me, which they also did, eyes downcast and shaking, spluttering mud. One of them was crying, snuffling through his snot and tears. Then he told them to beat it and they ran away, blubbering and tripping over their own feet.

I stared down at my savior as his unkempt hair fluttered in the breeze. He wore a Foo Fighters T-shirt under his leather jacket and his jeans were ripped, like mine. "You can go home now, you know," he said, like maybe I was slow.

I just sat there, picking dried mud from my jeans.

"Aren't your parents waiting?"

I didn't answer. I knew better than to answer questions like that.

When other kids found out what happened to Dad they either made fun of me or worse, they felt sorry for me. And Jesse said not to tell anyone Mom was sick again. He said if they knew how sick she was, they might take us away from her.

So I said, "I'm waiting for my brother."

He glanced around at the empty playground. "Who's your brother? And why isn't he here kicking those little shits up the ass?"

"Jesse," I said. "My brother is Jesse. He's in detention with Zane."

He took a step closer, teetering on the edge of the sandbox. "Yeah? How come?"

"They... um... got in an argument with Ms. Nielsen because she said I can't come to school in dirty clothes. They do that a lot," I mumbled, wishing maybe I hadn't said all that, except he looked kind of impressed about the detention thing.

He looked at my jeans; I'd gotten them muddy when I sat in a ditch to listen to music before school. I could pretend it didn't hurt me if he said something mean about it, but that didn't mean I wanted to hear it.

Why didn't he just go away?

"Well, you can come down. Those little shits aren't coming back."

I picked at the hole in the knee of my jeans, where my kneecap was poking through.

He leaned over, resting his elbows on Thunderdome. "What're you doing up there?"

"Playing Thunderdome."

I knew how stupid it sounded when no one else was there. It wasn't like I didn't have *any* friends to play with when my brother wasn't around, but they all had parents who picked them up after school. Anyway, I thought it might impress him. Thunderdome was outlawed by the teachers and we only played it after school.

He stepped into the sandbox. "How do you play?"

"It's quicksand!" I squealed. "You can't step in it!"

"Oh. Shit." He jumped up on the dome. "Almost lost a shoe." He looked up at me and his hair fell over his eye again. Blue; his eyes were a deep, dark blue. He climbed to the top of the dome and sat across from me.

Maybe he wasn't making fun of me; he just didn't know the rules of Thunderdome.

"It's okay," I told him. "You're safe up here with me. I'm the princess."

It was true; my brother and his friends always let me be the princess so I'd stay out of the way while they played, and sometimes they let me decide on the winner in case of a tie. But I figured it sounded more important if I left that out.

He pulled out a cigarette and lit it with a shiny flip-top lighter that had been scraped and dented all to hell, and started smoking. His hands were scraped too, his knuckles split and scabbed over. His fingernails were too short, chewed all down into the nail bed, his cuticles all ragged and blood-encrusted. They were a mess. But his face...

He was so… pretty.

"What happened to your hands?"

He didn't answer. Just smoked his cigarette and looked out across the school grounds, his arms wrapped around his knees, watching as parents picked their kids up in the distance, along the road in front of the school.

"A princess, huh?"

"*The* princess."

"So who's the prince, then?"

"Don't need one."

He looked at me. "Then who's gonna save you if you fall in the quicksand?"

"I will."

"What if you can't?"

"Then you can," I said. "If you want to. But you might get stuck in there, too."

He stared at me for a minute. Then he smiled, slowly, and it was like the sun coming out from behind the clouds.

"Then I guess we'll sink together." He took a couple of drags of his cigarette, his eyes squinting through the smoke. "You got a name, princess?"

"Jessa Mayes."

"Jessa Mayes," he repeated. "Don't ever let those little shits talk to you that way, yeah? Next time they try, you make a fist, like this." He showed me, clenching his fist until his split knuckles looked like they might burst. "And you hit 'em, right here, in the nose, as hard as you can. You do it hard enough, they'll go down. Then you run away. You do that once, they're not gonna bother you again."

I shook my head. "I'm not supposed to hit people. My brother says sticks and stones—"

"Yeah?" He flicked the ash off his cigarette and spat on the sand below. "Well, your brother's a pussy who doesn't know shit."

I gaped at him.

No one talked about Jesse like that. The other kids all thought he walked on water because he could play guitar.

"I can't make a fifth-grader eat crap." My face was getting hot and I looked down at the sand. "Maybe you can. I can't."

When I glanced up again, he was taking something off his jacket. He held it out to me. "Take it," he said.

I took it from his outstretched hand and examined it. It was a little silver pin shaped like a motorcycle. It said *Sinners MC* on a banner that wrapped around the tires. There was a woman on the motorcycle but she wasn't riding it, exactly. She was facing the wrong way and reclined back, her back arched, shoving her boobs out.

I was eight.

I had no idea what *Sinners MC* meant, so it never occurred to me to wonder why he had a pin that belonged to an outlaw motorcycle club.

"You wear that," he said, glancing over my shoulder, "no one's gonna mess with you." He was looking in the direction of the school, his eyes narrowing as he dragged on his cigarette.

"Smoking on school grounds *again* Mr. Mason?"

I turned to find a teacher stalking toward us, one of those shit-eating bullies in tow, red-faced, looking anywhere but at us. "What will your parents have to say about this?"

"Can't wait to find out," he muttered. His blue eyes met mine as he tossed his cigarette aside. Then he smiled at me again.

I smiled back.

He leapt to the ground, jumping over the quicksand and landing in the grass.

"See you around, princess."

I watched him shove his hands in the pockets of his jeans and walk away. But it wasn't true; I didn't see him around. He never even came back to school after that day.

Not for two whole years.

Those bullies never bothered me again, though. None of them did. And I was pretty sure it wasn't because of some pin. It was because of *him*.

Because he'd made two fifth-graders eat shit for being mean to me, and no one wanted to eat shit.

The next year, when a new girl in my class asked me about my motorcycle pin, she didn't believe me when I told her where I'd gotten it. As if I'd made up the whole thing about the badass boy in the leather jacket who saved me from a couple of bullies— then mysteriously vanished from school, never to return—just to impress her.

But I knew he was real.

I had his pin, and I had his picture. In the seventh grade class photo in the school yearbook he was standing right next to my brother, staring down the lens of the camera like he was ready to take on the world… and make it eat shit.

His name was Brody Mason.

He was the love of my life.

If only I'd figured that out a lot sooner than I did.

Made in the USA
Coppell, TX
05 December 2024

41782514R00100